Charles G.

The Ingoldsby Country

Charles G. Harper

The Ingoldsby Country

1st Edition | ISBN: 978-3-75234-179-9

Place of Publication: Frankfurt am Main, Germany

Year of Publication: 2020

Outlook Verlag GmbH, Germany.

THE INGOLDSBY COUNTRY

BY

CHARLES G. HARPER

"Ingoldsby" has always been of that comparatively small number of authors who command a personal interest and affection. Reading the *"Legends"* you cannot choose but see that when he sat down, often at the midnight hour, to dash off the fun and frolic that came so readily to his mind, it was a part of himself that appeared upon the page. He did not and could not, when he wrote for publication under a pseudonym, be other than himself, and did not self-consciously draw a veil of style around him and speak, a cloaked figure lacking ordinary human attributes, or as other than a man of the world. He claimed no sacerdotal privileges, and we know, from the published "Life and Letters" by his son, that he was in his life and intimacies, as the Reverend R. H. Barham, the same genial wit and humorist he appeared as *"Tom Ingoldsby."* He must, therefore, have been a likeable man, and those who knew him were fortunate persons. The next best thing to knowing him is to know something of the Ingoldsby Country, that corner of Kent where he was born and whose legends he has put to such splendid literary uses. The *"Ingoldsby Legends"* have so long since become a classic that it is indeed somewhat surprising that no literary pilgrim, for love of their author and interest in his career, has before this traced the landmarks of his storied district.

CHARLES G. HARPER.

Petersham, Surrey.
January, 1904.

CHAPTER I

INTRODUCTORY

The present writer foregathered a little while since with a man who had been to the uttermost parts of the earth. He had just returned from Australia, and was casually met on what the vulgar call the "Tuppenny Tube," travelling from the Bank to Shepherd's Bush. It was a humorous anti-climax to all those other journeys, but that is not the point here to be made. He was full, as might have been expected, of tales strange and curious of those outposts of civilisation he had visited, and of legends of places—whose names generally ended with two gulps and a click—where civilisation was an unknown quantity. But to this man, who had been everywhere and elsewhere, who had crossed the Dark Continent when it was still dark, England, his native land, was largely a sealed book. Even as one spoke with him it could be perceived how perfect an exemplar he was of many globe-trotting Britons who roam the world and can talk to you at first hand of Bulawayo or the Australian bush, but are instantly nonplussed if the subject of rural England be broached.

When he was done talking of places with savage and infinitely-repetitive names, composed of fantastically-arranged vowels, with never a consonant to consort with them, he was asked if he knew Kent. "Kent?" he repeated, in Jingle-like fashion, "why, yes. Canterbury Cathedral, hop-gardens, Charles Dickens, Rochester, Dover, and—and all that," he concluded, with a vague sweep of his arm. "Run through it on y'r way to Paris," he added, in an explanatory way. And that was all he knew of Kent: a place you run through, on the way to somewhere else! a country observed from fleeting and not very attentive glances obtained from a railway-carriage window! Such glances furnished him fully forth in all he had cared to know of the Garden of England!

Not that one fully subscribes to that familiar epithet of praise, which must have originally been given by a Cockney who knew no better. Who that ever has sojourned in the west, and has known lovely Devon, would for a moment give Kent that pride of place? Now, if it were called the "Market Garden of England——!" What?

But this is not to say that Kent is not very beautiful; only it is not Devon. I do not pillory Kent because it is not something else, and would by no means contemn its chalky soil because of any affection for the good red earth of that other shire. Kent has its lovable qualities, and when you have eliminated the thronging tramps, the paper and other factories, the objectionable hop-pickers, the beanfeasters, and the multitudinous yahoos who people its nearer Cockneyfied districts, there is a very considerable residuum of exquisite country. The elimination of all those items would be what the slangy term a "big order"; but the tourist who knows, and even the tourist who does not actually *know*, but can infer and deduce, need never lose himself in the Kent of commerce and blackguardism. He seeks out, and by instinct finds, the best; and, having found the best that Kent affords, is ready to declare that it is hard to beat. It is, for example, impossible to match, even in Devon, the beauty of that fertile fruit and hop-bearing belt of country which begins at Newington, a few miles below Chatham, and continues beside the Dover Road, past Teynham and Faversham, and on to Canterbury. It is a beauty that appeals alike and at once to the artist and the man with carnal appetites and fleshly longings; for, once off the dusty high-road, it is a constant succession of orchards and hop-gardens, wherein it is pleasant to lie on sunny afternoons in the dappled shade of the apple, pear, or cherry-trees, with the swede-eating sheep for sole companions, and the noise of the toilsome world coming restfully over the hedgerows.

It *is* a noisy and a toilsome world. There goes the roar of the big guns down at the Medway forts; the clear note of the bugles sings up faintly—like an anthem from amid a naughty nest of vipers—out of Chatham and New Brompton (we are being duly taken care of!); the whistling and rushing of the railway trains are never still, and you can hear that holiday world which takes its vacation strenuously, "pip-pipping" on cycles, "poop-pooping" on motor-cars, and playing the yearnful concertina on the passing break like anything, t'other side of the merciful hedge. Even if you could not hear them, the signs of their passing would be evident in the cloud of chalk-dust which, like the pillar of cloud by day that guided the Children of Israel, marks their route. But the Land of Promise sought by those pilgrims, at such speed, is not ours. How should it be? Theirs is ever the Next Place; ours is Here. Theirs is the Promise without fruition; ours is granted to the full, and Now, wherever we be. That is if we be indeed wise in our generation, and content with the happy moment. One understands that same happy moment, here and now, to be passed in the consumption of ripe cherries out of a cool cabbage-leaf, in the shade of the boughs that bore them. This is one way in which beauteous Kent appeals, as we have said, to the carnal man, who perceives that if indeed Devonshire cream be good, equally good are the kindly fruits of Kent.

If Kent be essentially the Market Garden of England, rather than pre-eminently the Garden in the picturesque sense, certainly this country yields to none other in historic or literary interest. That coast where Cæsar and Augustine, easily first among the great personages of history, landed; this fertile county which contains the Metropolitan Cathedral of the Church of

England; the neighbourhood of Rochester and Maidstone, linked with the literary activities of Charles Dickens, must needs hold the affections of Englishmen, irrespective of the physical and æsthetic attractions of scenery. But there is another great literary figure connected with Kent, both by birth and by reason of his having exploited many of its rural legends in his merry verse. Richard Harris Barham was born at Canterbury, and in his *Ingoldsby Legends* created an Ingoldsby Country, which he had already peopled with many notable characters before death cut him off in his prime. The capital of the Ingoldsby Country is Canterbury; its very heart and core is comprised within the district to the east of a line drawn due south from Whitstable to Canterbury, Denton, and Hythe; and its frontiers make an indeterminate line to the west, beyond Romney Marsh and Ashford. The whole north coast of Kent, including Sheppey, the Swale, and the littoral of the Thames and Medway, is part and parcel of Ingoldsby Land, whose isolated and far-off dependencies are found at Shrewsbury, the scene of "Bloudie Jack"; or Salisbury Plain, where the "Dead Drummer" is located; at Wayland Wood, near Wymondham, in Norfolk, where the legend of the "Babes in the Wood" belongs; and at Netley Abbey, the scene of a fine poem. London, too, has its Ingoldsby associations, duly set forth in these pages.

THE INGOLDSBY COUNTRY

CHAPTER II

BARHAM: THE AUTHOR OF THE *INGOLDSBY LEGENDS*

There are *coteries*, circles inner and outer, in the world of letters, and there have always been. There are some in this time of ours whose members think they are of the giants whose memory the world will not willingly let die. There were other *coterie* when the nineteenth century was but newly come into its second quarter, when the period that is now known as Early Victorian was in the making, and when the Queen was young. The members of those literary brotherhoods are gone, each one to his place, and the memories of the most of them, of the books they wrote, the jokes they cracked, of their friendships and quarrels, are dim and dusty to-day. The taste in humour and pathos is not the taste of this time, which laughs at the pathos, and finds the humour, when not dull, merely spiteful and vindictive. When you rise from a perusal of Douglas Jerrold's wounding wit, you think him ungenerous and a cad, De Quincey's frolics merely elephantine, Hood's facilities dull, and Leigh Hunt's performances but journalism.

All this is but the foil to show the brilliant humour, the fun, and the truly pathetic note of Richard Harris Barham's writings to better effect. Time has breathed upon the glass through which we see the lives and performances of Barham's contemporaries, and has obscured our view of them; but the author of the *Ingoldsby Legends* remains, almost alone among that Early Victorian band, as acceptable to-day (nay, perhaps even more acceptable) than he was fifty years ago.

The *Ingoldsby Legend* will never be allowed to die. Indeed, we live in times when their admirable sanity might well be invoked as a counterblast to modern neurotic conditions, and a healthy revulsion from superstitious revivals. Written at that now historic time when the Ritualistic innovations and tendency towards Roman Catholicism of the new school of theology at Oxford were agitating English thought, they express the common-sense scorn of the healthy mind against the mystification and deceit of the religion that the Reformation pitched, neck and crop, out of England, close upon three hundred and seventy years ago, and for which the large-minded tolerance of to-day is not enough. Domination is its aim, but no mind that can enjoy the mirth and marvels of the Legends has any room for such ghostly pretensions, and their continued popularity is thus, by parity of reasoning, something of an assurance. The *Ingoldsby Legends* are included in the *Index Expurgatorium* of Rome.

Superfine critics have in recent years declared that Barham's fun has grown out of date, and that they cannot read him as of old. But your critic commonly speaks only for himself; and moreover, the superfine, who cannot read Dickens, for example, have been sadly flouted of late by the still increasing popular favour of that novelist.

It was in the fertile county of Kent that Barham was born, in the midst of a district that has ever been the cradle of Barhams. Eight miles to the south of the old Cathedral of Canterbury, and near by the Folkestone Road, there lies, secluded in a deep valley, an old-fashioned farmhouse, unpretending enough to the outward glance, but quaint and curious within. This is the old manor house of Tappington Everard, mentioned so often and so familiarly in the *Ingoldsby Legend*, and for many centuries the home of Richard Harris Barham's ancestors. "Tom Ingoldsby" himself was, indeed, born at Canterbury, near the Cathedral precincts, and first saw the world beneath the shadow of that great Church, of whose glories he was in after years to tell in his own peculiar and inimitable way. His father, made rich by hops, was a man of consideration at Canterbury, and filled an Aldermanic chair with all the dignity that comes of adipose tissue largely developed. He was, in fact and few words, a fat man, and it was probably in reference to him that Tom Ingoldsby, in later years, wrote of the "aldermanic nose" trumpeting in the Cathedral during service.

The Rev. Richard Harris Barham, the self-styled "Thomas Ingoldsby", claimed descent from the De Bearhams, anciently the FitzUrses, whose possessions extended round about Tappington for many miles of this fair county of Kent. He delighted to think that he was descended from one of those four knights who, on that dark December day of 1170, broke in upon the religious quiet of the Cathedral and slaughtered Becket in the north transept. When their crime was wrought the murderers fled, FitzUrse escaping to Ireland, where he is said to have taken the name of MacMahon, the Irish equivalent of his original patronymic, which was just the Norman-Latin for "Bear's Son".

He died an exile, leaving his Manor of Barham to his brother, who, so odious had the name of FitzUrse now become, changed it for an Anglicised variant, and called himself "De Bearham." Eventually the aristocratic prefix "De" fell out of use, and in course of time even Bearham became "Barham."

The Barhams held place and power here for centuries, giving their name to the village of Barham, which nestles, embowered in foliage, beneath the bleak and bare expanse of Barham Downs; their estates dropping from them little by little until, in the time of James I., the remaining property was alienated by a Thomas Barham, a nerveless, unworthy descendant of the fierce FitzUrses, who sold it to the Reverend Charles Fotherby, Archdeacon of Canterbury. Thus were the Barhams torn from their native soil and rendered landless.

The adjoining manor of Tappington, next Barham, had been held in 1272 by one Gerrard de Tappington, as one knight's fee. In the reign of Henry VIII. it was purchased by a certain John Boys, who died in 1544, when his son, William Boys, alienated a small portion of the demesne to a person named Verrier, and the manor, with the remainder of the demesne, to one Marsh, to whose descendants it passed until at length sold by Colonel Thomas Marsh to Mr. Thomas Harris, hopfactor of Canterbury, who died in 1729, and whose daughter and sole heiress had, by a singular freak of fate, married a John Barham, bringing him not only the old manor of Tappington, or Tapton Wood, as it has sometimes been styled, as her dower, but also some portions of the long-lost lands of those whom he claimed for ancestors, including the manors of Parmstead (called in olden times Barhamstead).

It will be noted that it was a John Barham—not necessarily one of the Barhams of Tappington—who thus secured the Harris heiress. Kent contains more than one family of the name, but let us hope, for the sake of sentiment, that all Barhams, of whatever district, descend from the original assassin. It would certainly have been a grievous thing to Tom Ingoldsby if he had been compelled to cherish a doubt of the blood-boltered genuineness of his own ancestry. We have, indeed, some slightly different versions of what became of the FitzUrse family. One tells us that a branch lingered long in the neighbourhood of Williton, in Somerset, under their proper name, which became successively corrupted into Fitzour, and Fishour, and at last assumed the common form of Fisher. This is good news for Fishers anxious to assume long descent, even if they have to date from a murderer. Time throws an historic condonation over such things, and many an ambitious person who would not willingly kill a fly, and who would very naturally shrink from owning any connection with a homicidal criminal now on his trial, would glow with pride at an attested family tree springing from that blood-thirsty knight.

Another tales gives the Italian name of Orsini as a variant of FitzUrse. If there be anything in it, then assuredly the notorious Orsini of the infernal machine, who attempted the life of Napoleon III., was a reversion to twelfth century type.

Other Barhams there are known to fame: Henry, surgeon and natural history writer, who died in 1726, and was one of the family of Barhams of Barham Court; and Nicholas Barham, lawyer, of Wadhurst, Sussex, who died in 1577, and was descended from the Barhams of Teston, near Maidstone. Nicholas was ever a favourite Christian name with all branches of the family, and Tom

Ingoldsby so named his youngest son—the "Little Boy Ned" of the Legends.

The witty and mirth-provoking Reverend Richard Harris Barham, destined to bear the most distinguished name of all his race, was fourth in descent from the peculiarly fortunate John Barham who wedded the Harris hopfields and the Harris daughter. His father, himself a "Richard Harris" Barham—was that alderman of capacious paunch of whom mention has already been made. He resided at 61, Burgate Street, Canterbury, a large, substantial house of pallid grey brick, plain almost to ugliness outside, but remarkably comfortable and beautifully appointed within, standing at the corner of Canterbury Lane. A brick of the garden wall facing the lane may be observed, scratched lightly with "M. B. 1733."

To this house he had succeeded on the death of his father, Richard Barham, in 1784. He did not very long enjoy the inheritance.

Thos Ingoldsby

"TOM INGOLDSBY": THE REV. RICHARD HARRIS BARHAM.

From a drawing by his son, the Rev. Richard Harris Dalton Barham.

The alderman was of truly aldermanic proportions, for he weighed nineteen stone. Existing portraits of him introduce us to a personage of a more than

Falstaffian appearance, and the tale is still told how it was found necessary to widen the doorway at the time of his funeral. For eleven years he lived here; and here it was, December 6th, 1788, that the only child of himself and his housekeeper, Elizabeth Fox, was born.

Elizabeth Fox came from Minster-in-Thanet. A miniature portrait of her shows a fair-haired, bright-eyed woman, with abundant indications of a sunny nature, rich in wit and humour. It is quite clear that it was from his mother Ingoldsby derived his mirthful genius, just as in a companion miniature of himself, painted at the age of six, representing him as a pretty, vivacious little boy with large brown roguish eyes, he bore a striking likeness to her.

It is singular to note that the future rector of St. Mary Magdalene in the City of London was as an infant baptised at a church of precisely the same dedication—that of St. Mary Magdalene in Burgate Street, a few doors only removed from his birthplace. The tower only of that church is now standing, the rest having been pulled down in 1871. It is still possible to decipher some of the tablets fixed against the wall of the tower, but exposed to the weather and slowly decaying. There is one to Ingoldsby's grandfather, Richard, who died December 11th, 1784, aged 82, and to his grandmother, Elizabeth Barham, who died October 2nd, 1781, aged 81; and other tablets commemorate his aunts Eliza and Sarah, who died September 26th, 1782, and December 16th, 1784, aged respectively forty-six and forty-four years.

THE HOUSE, 61, BURGATE STREET, CANTERBURY, WHERE THE AUTHOR OF THE "INGOLDSBY LEGENDS" WAS BORN.

ST. MARY MAGDALENE, BURGATE STREET, CANTERBURY.

Ingoldsby was only in his seventh year when a very serious thing befell, for his father, the alderman, died in 1795. Those who love their Ingoldsby and everything that was his, as the present writer does, will be interested to know that he was buried at Upper Hardres ("Hards," in the Kentish speech), a small and lonely village, four miles from Canterbury, on the old Stone Street, as you go towards Lympne and Hythe. There, in the village church, high up on the south wall of the nave, the tablet to his memory may be found. What became of Elizabeth Fox is beyond our ken. We are told, in the *Life and Letters of Richard Harris Barham*, by his son the Reverend Richard Dalton Barham, that she was at the time a confirmed invalid.

THE HALL, 61, BURGATE STREET, CANTERBURY, WHERE THE AUTHOR OF THE
"INGOLDSBY LEGENDS" WAS BORN.

To three guardians had been given the administration of the comfortable patrimony of the boy, and by them he was sent to St. Paul's School, then in the City of London. Thence he went to Brasenose, Oxford, leaving the university with a modest B.A., degree in 1811. Meanwhile the villain of the piece had been at work, in the person of a dishonest attorney, one of his guardians, by whose practices his fortune was very seriously reduced. Returning to Canterbury, he seems to have contemplated studying for the law, but quickly relinquished the idea, and prepared himself for the Church. He was admitted to holy orders, and in 1813, in his twenty-fifth year obtained a curacy at Ashford. This was exchanged in the following year for the curacy of the neighbouring village of Westwell. Thus he was fairly launched on his professional career, becoming successively Rector of Snargate and Curate of Warehorne, Minor Canon of St. Paul's and Rector of the united parishes of St. Mary Magdalene with St. Gregory-by-St.-Paul's, and finally, by exchange in 1842, Rector of St. Faith-by-St.-Paul's—a fine mid-nineteenth century specimen of the "squarson." A competent genealogist, an accomplished antiquary, a man of letters, he, by force of his sprightly wit, welded the fragmentary legends of the country—but largely those of his native county of Kent—into those astonishing amalgams of fact and fiction which, published first, from time to time, in *Bentley's Miscellany*, were collected and issued as the *Ingoldsby Legends*. It is not the least among the charms of those verses that fact and fiction are so inextricably mixed in them that it needs the learning of the skilled antiquary to sift the one from the other; and so plausible are many of his ostensible citations from old Latin documents, and his fictitious genealogies so interwoven with the names, the marriages and descents of persons, real and imaginary, that an innocent who wrote some years ago to *Notes and Queries*, desiring further particulars of what he thought to be genuine records, is surely to be excused for his too-ready faith.

The assumed name of "Ingoldsby" is stated by his son to be found in a branch of the family genealogy, but inquiry fails to trace the name in that connection, and it may be said at once that the Kentish Ingoldsbys are entirely figments of Barham's lively imagination. Yorkshire knows a family of that name, of whom Barham probably had never heard anything save their name. He was a man of property, and modestly proud of the descent he claimed, and though by no means rich, his place was among—

> The *élite* of the old county families round,
> Such as Honeywood, Oxenden, Knatchbull and Norton,
> Matthew Robinson, too, with his beard, from Monk's Horton,
> The Faggs, and Finch-Hattons, Tokes, Derings, and Deedses,
> And Fairfax (who then called the castle of Leeds his).

He was, in fact, "armigerous", as heralds would say, and the arms of his family were—not those lioncels of the Shurlands impaled with the saltire of the Ingoldsbys, of which we may read in the Legends—but as pictured here. It may be noted that another Barham family—the Barhams of Teston, near Maidstone—bore the three bears for arms, without the distinguishing fesse; and that they are shown thus on an old brass plate in Ashford church, which Ingoldsby must often have seen during his early curacy there.

THE BARHAM COAT-OF-ARMS.

When, however, he talks of the escutcheons displayed in the great hall of Tappington, charged with the armorial bearings of the family and its connections, he does more than to picturesquely embroider facts. He invents them, and the "old coat" "in which a *chevron between three eagles' cuisses sable* is blazoned quarterly with the *engrailed saltire* of the Ingoldsbys"— which Mr. Simpkinson found to be that of "Sir Ingoldsby Bray, *temp.* Richard I."—is one not known to the Heralds' College.

Behind that farcical "Mr. Simpkinson, from Bath," lurks a real person, and one not unknown to those who have read Britton and Brayley books on Cathedral antiquities. John Britton, the original of Simpkinson, was, equally with his contemporary Barham, an antiquary and genealogist of accomplishment, and a herald of repute. Barham would not have allowed as much, for there was, it would seem, a certain amount of ill-feeling between the two, which resulted in the satirical passages relating to "Mr. Simpkinson" to be met with in the pages of the *Ingoldsby Legends*. They tell us that he was, among other things, "an influential member of the Antiquarian Society, to whose 'Beauties of Bagnigge Wells' he had been a liberal subscriber"; and that "his inaugural essay on the President's cocked-hat was considered a miracle of erudition; and his account of the earliest application of gilding to gingerbread a masterpiece of antiquarian research." In all this one finds something of that rapier-thrust of satire, that mordant wit which comes of personal rivalry; and the heartfelt scorn of a man who loved architecture, and was, indeed, a member of the first Archæological Institute, but who whole-heartedly resented the introduction of picnic parties into archæological excursions, and revolted at popularising architecture and antiquarian research by brake parties, in which the popping of champagne corks punctuated the remarks of speakers holding forth on the architectural features of buildings in a style sufficiently picturesque and simple to hold the attention of the ladies. Those who have found how unconquerable is the indifference of the public to these things will appreciate to the fullest extent the feelings of Tom Ingoldsby, while yet reserving some meed of admiration for John Britton's labours, which did much to advance the slow-growing knowledge of Gothic architecture in the first half of the century. His work may halt somewhat, his architectural knowledge be something piecemeal and uninformed with inner light; but by his labours many others were led to pursue the study of ecclesiastical art.

But the humour with which Barham surrounded "Mr. Simpkinson's" doings took no count of his accomplishments, as may be seen in the excursion to "Bolsover Priory", narrated in "The Spectre of Tappington". "Bolsover Priory", said Mr. Simpkinson, "was founded in the reign of Henry VI. about the beginning of the eleventh century. Hugh de Bolsover had accompanied that monarch to the Holy Land, in the expedition undertaken by way of penance for the murder of his young nephews in the Tower. Upon the dissolution of the monasteries, the veteran was enfeoffed in the lands and manor, to which he gave his own name of Bolsover, or Bee-Owls-Over (by corruption Bolsover)—a Bee in chief over Three Owls, all proper, being the armorial ensigns borne by this distinguished crusader at the siege of Acre."

Thus far Simpkinson. Now Barham turns, with good effect, on the ignorant sightseers to whom ruins are just a curiosity and nothing more.

"'Ah! that was Sir Sidney Smith,' said Mr. Peters; 'I've heard tell of him, and all about Mrs. Partington, and—'

"'P., be quiet, and don't expose yourself!' sharply interrupted his lady. P. was silenced, and betook himself to the bottled stout.

"'These lands,' continued the antiquary, 'were held in grand sergeantry by the presentation of three white owls and a pot of honey——'

"'Lassy me! how nice!' said Miss Julia. Mr. Peters licked his lips.

"'Pray give me leave, my dear—owls and honey, whenever the king should come a-rat-catching in this part of the country.'

"'Rat-catching!' ejaculated the Squire, pausing abruptly in the mastication of a drum-stick.

"'To be sure, my dear sir; don't you remember that rats once came under the forest laws—a minor species of venison? "Rats and mice, and such small deer," eh?—Shakespeare, you know. Our ancestors ate rats; and owls, you know, are capital mousers——'

"'I seen a howl,' said Mr. Peters."

"Bolsover Priory" is one of those few places mentioned by Ingoldsby that have not been identified with any real place in Kent. It might have been taken to mean the ruins of the Preceptory at Swingfield Minnis, some two miles from Tappington, had not Barham expressly said, in his prefatory notes to the "Witches' Frolic," that they were not the same.

ST. PAUL'S CHURCHYARD, DEMOLISHED 1901.

The literary landmarks associated with Barham's residence in London are readily traced. On leaving Kent in 1821 to take up his residence in London, he, for a time, rented the upper part of the house, still standing, No. 51, Great Queen Street, Holborn. There his eldest surviving daughter, Caroline Frances Barham, afterwards Lady Bond, was born, July 22nd, 1823. In 1824, following his appointment to the rectorship of St. Mary Magdalene, the family removed to a house numbered "4" on the south side of St. Paul's churchyard, and there remained until 1839, when an exchange was made to a house in Amen Corner, Paternoster Row—the first house through the gateway —by arrangement with Sydney Smith, who was leaving it to reside in Green Street, Mayfair.

He describes the garden at the back of this house as "containing three polyanthus roots, a real tree, a brown box border, a snuff-coloured jessamine, a shrub which is either a dwarf acacia or an overgrown gooseberry bush, eight broken bottles, and a tortoise-shell tom-cat asleep in the sunniest corner, with a wide and extensive prospect of the back of the 'Oxford Arms,' and a fine *hanging* wood (the 'new drop' at Newgate) in the distance."

18

AMEN CORNER, WHERE BARHAM DIED.

But the sprightly wit, the sound common-sense, the good-natured satire, were doomed to early extinction. It was in the prime of life, and when he might well have looked forward to further consolidating and extending the fame his genius had already brought, that the blow fell which laid him low. He had already, some twenty years earlier, suffered some slight temporary trouble with a sensitive throat, and although in general a robust man, was in that respect peculiarly liable to the weather. It happened, unfortunately, that he was present as a spectator at the opening by the Queen of the new Royal Exchange, October 28th, 1844. It was a bleak day, and, sitting at an open window in Cheapside placed at his disposal by a friend, he caught a chill from whose effects he never recovered. The evil was a stubborn inflammation of the throat, which clung to him throughout the winter, and by degrees reduced the strong man to an alarmingly weak condition. In the February of 1845 he was induced to visit Bath, in the hope of recovery in that mild atmosphere, but an imprudent return to London in the treacherous month of March, in order to attend a meeting of the Archæological Association, aggravated the malady. Still, that strong physique struggled against illness, and he once more partly recovered, only to be again laid low by a cold caught at an April vestry meeting in St. Paul's. It was, however, not merely an exaggerated susceptibility to cold that by this time dogged his every excursion into the open air, but the grossly mistaken treatment of his medical man, who had inflamed the malady by applying caustic to the uvula. At the beginning of May, although reduced almost to the condition of a helpless child by his sufferings, he was taken again to the west; this time to Clifton, near Bristol. Unhappily, the local practitioner who was called in to attend him was by no means a properly qualified man, and on hearing of the mistaken treatment already followed, could think of nothing better than to continue it. It is not remarkable, under the circumstances, that he experienced no relief from the climate of Clifton, but grew steadily weaker. It was a sad time, for his wife was simultaneously laid low with illness. Everything devolved upon his daughter, Frances, then only in her twentieth year, for his son Dick was away in Cambridgeshire, doing duty as a clergyman.

RUINS OF ST. MARY MAGDALENE, OLD FISH STREET HILL, CITY OF LONDON, AFTER THE FIRE OF DECEMBER 1886.

The dying man—for the truth could be no longer disguised—kept a spirit of the supremest cheerfulness and Christian courage. His humorous verses on the incidents of his distressing illness—originally composed as replies to the inquiries of anxious friends and afterwards published in the collection of *Ingoldsby Lyrics* as "The Bulletin," are no whit inferior to the productions of his careless health.

When recovery at Clifton seemed hopeless, he was removed again to London, to the house he had occupied for the last six years, and made a grim joke as they assisted him into the house, on the appropriateness of his being brought at that juncture to Amen Corner. A few days he lay there, life ebbing away from sheer weakness; his mind still clear, and divided between making the most careful disposition of his property and fond memories of that "little boy Ned" who had died, untimely, some years before. It was then he wrote that last poem, the beautiful "As I Laye a-thynkynge," printed at the end of all editions of the *Ingoldsby Legends* as "The Last Lines of Thomas Ingoldsby." There is not, to my mind, anything more exquisitely beautiful and pathetic in the gorgeous roll of English literature than the seven stanzas of the swan-song of this master of humour and pathos. It is wholly for themselves, and not by reason of reading into them the special circumstances under which they were written, that so sweeping a judgment is made. That they have never been properly recognised is due to the Wardour Street antiquity of their spelling, and still more to that strange insistence which ordains that the accepted wit and humourist must always be "funny" or go unacknowledged. It is a strange penalty; one that would seek to deprive the humourist of all human emotions save that of laughter, and so make him that reproach of honest men—a cynic.

It was on June 17th, 1845, that Barham died, untimely, before the completion of his fifty-seventh year. He was buried in the vaults of his former church, St. Mary Magdalene, Old Fish Street Hill, one of those half-deserted city churches built by Sir Christopher Wren after the Great Fire of London. There he might have lain until now, but for the fire of December 2nd, 1886, which destroyed the building. For at least four years the blackened and roofless ruins stood, fronting Knightrider Street, and then they were removed, to make way for warehouses. The contents of the vaults were at the same time dispersed, the remains of Tom Ingoldsby being removed to Kensal Green Cemetery, while the tablet to his memory was appropriately transferred to St. Paul's, where, in the crypt, it may still be seen.

CHAPTER III

CANTERBURY

There stands a city, neither large nor small,
Its air and situation sweet and pretty.
It matters very little, if at all,
Whether its denizens are dull or witty;
Whether the ladies there are short or tall,
Brunettes or blondes; only, there stands a city!
Perhaps 'tis also requisite to minute,
That there's a Castle and a Cobbler in it.

Thus wrote Ingoldsby of his native city of Canterbury, in "The Ghost," and "sweet and pretty" its air and situation remain, sixty years since those lines were penned. For the changes that have altered so many other cities and towns have brought little disturbance here. No manufactures have come to abolish the prettiness of the situation; the air—the atmospheric air—is sweet and fragrant as of yore, and that other air—the demeanour and deportment—of Canterbury is still, as ever, gravely cheerful, as surely befits the capital city of a Primate whose Church is still a going concern.

Ingoldsby was exactly right in his epithetical summing-up, for prettiness and not grandeur is the characteristic of the gentle valley of the Stour, wherein Canterbury is set. Approach it from whatever quarter you will, and you will find prettiness only in the situation. Even when viewed from the commanding heights of Harbledown and St. Thomas's Hill, the only grandeur is that of the Cathedral, and that is extrinsic, a something imported into the picture. Nay, even the uprising bulk of that cathedral church gains in effect from being thus set down in midst of a valley that is almost with equal justness called a plain, and whose features may, without offence, or the suspicion of any thought derogatory from their beauty, be termed so featureless.

Unquestionably the best direction whence to enter this ancient capital of the Kentish folk—this Kaintware-bury of the Saxons, the Durovernum of the Romans—is from Harbledown, whence the pilgrims from London, or from the north and west of England, entered. Only thus does the stranger receive a really accurate impression. With emotions doubtless less violent than those of the mediæval pilgrims to the shrine of the blessed martyr, St. Thomas, but still strongly aroused, he sees the west front of the Cathedral, its two western "towers," and the great central "Bell-Harry" tower displayed boldly before him, in the level, and may even identify the more prominent of the public buildings. Descending from this hill, he passes through the ancient suburb of Saint Dunstan, and enters the city beneath the frowning portals of the West Gate.

If, on the other hand, the modern pilgrim arrives per Chatham and Dover Railway, he will be dumped down in quite a different direction, on the south side of the city, near Wincheap Street, in which thoroughfare he will be able, without any delay, to discover his first Ingoldsby landmark in Canterbury, in the shape of the "Harris's Almshouses," founded in 1729 by that ancestral Harris whose daughter his great-grandfather had married. They are five quite humble little red-brick houses, with a garden at the back, endowed for the support of two poor parishioners of St. Mary Magdalene, two of Thanington, and one of St. Mildred's. The value is the modest one of about £9 a year. An unassuming tablet on the central house of the row tells this story:

> Mr. Thomas Harris
> of this City
> Founder of these Five
> Alms-Houses
> hath endowed them with
> Marly Farm in Kent
> for the Maintenance of five
> Poor Familys for ever.

Ingoldsby—the Reverend Richard Harris Barham—became a governor of this charity on his attaining his majority, as already alluded to in the sketch of his birth and career.

The district of Wincheap only becomes tolerable after leaving the railway behind. This outlying part, without the city walls, was of old that place of degradation where the scourgings and stripes, the whips and scorpions of mediæval punishments, were inflicted; where offending books—ay, and the horror of it, the Protestant martyrs—were burnt of yore. In this "Potter's Field" that is not now more than a struggling little suburb where all the littlenesses of life are prominent, and few of its beauties are to be seen, there has of late been erected a great granite memorial pillar, surmounted by the "Canterbury Cross," on the site of the stake at which forty-one victims of the Marian persecution perished. Shackle and stake, faggot and gyve, rivet and torch, how busy they were! It is a beautiful sentiment that rears this monument on the spot where they suffered who testified for Jesus; but it should stand, plain for all men to see, in the Cathedral Close itself.

Our course from this point into the city leads up to the Castle, mentioned in the Legends, and especially in that early one, "The Ghost," in whose stanzas are found many exquisitely apposite local Canterbury touches. That Castle is, in its secular way, as interesting as the Cathedral in its ecclesiastical:

> The Castle was a huge and antique mound,
>   Proof against all the artillery of the quiver,
> Ere those abominable guns were found,
>   To send cold lead through gallant warrior's liver.
> It stands upon a gently-rising ground,
>   Sloping down gradually to the river,
> Resembling (to compare great things with smaller)
>   A well-scoop'd, mouldy Stilton cheese—but taller.
>
> The Keep, I find, 's been sadly alter'd lately,
>   And, 'stead of mail-clad knights, of honour jealous,
> In martial panoply so grand and stately,
>   Its walls are fill'd with money-making fellows,
> And stuff'd, unless I'm misinformed greatly,
>   With leaden pipes, and coke, and coals, and bellows,
> In short, so great a change has come to pass,
> 'Tis now a manufactory of Gas.

CANTERBURY CASTLE.

It is immediately fronting the street that this keep of old romantic Norman times is found, with the smoke and noxious fumes, the chimneys and retorts, of the City of Canterbury Gas-light and Coke Company, very insistent to eyes and nose, in the rear; and, if you look down a by-street—"Gas Street" is the vulgar name of it—and peer into the empty roofless shell of that keep, you will discover it to be still a coal-bunker, and that those who, in the rhyme of Ingoldsby, manufacture "garss," are not more gentle with historic ruins than they were in 1825, when it was first put to this use. These shattered walls that, quarried by time and the hands of spoilers, do indeed, as Ingoldsby suggests,

25

resemble one of those great, well-scooped cheeses found in the coffee-rooms of old-fashioned hotels, were built by two very great castle-builders; by Gundulf, Bishop of Rochester, and William de Corbeil, Archbishop of Canterbury. What Gundulf began for his master and over-lord William the Conqueror, William de Corbeil completed for Henry I. Among all the great castle keeps of England it ranked third in size, and in that respect was inferior only to those of Colchester and Norwich. It looks a very poor third indeed nowadays, and so battered and reduced that a hundred keeps are more upstanding and impressive. Alas! for that poor castle, its career was never an heroic one. It surrendered tamely to Louis, the Dauphin of France, in 1216, and for long years afterwards was a prison for Jews on occasions when persecutions of the Chosen People broke out. From that use it declined to the lower level of a debtor's prison.

Not far distant from it are the Dane John gardens, a public park of by no means recent origin. It has been for more than a hundred years what it is now, and is perhaps one of the very best wooded and most picturesque urban parks in existence. Antiquaries have long since ceased to trouble about the odd name, which appears to have originally come from an estate here, belonging to the Castle, and variously named the "Castle" or "Donjon" Manor. The huge prehistoric mound within its area was remodelled, heaped seventeen feet higher, crowned with a monument that halts between Gothic and Classic, and ringed round with a spiral walk about 1790. The very long and very complacent statement on that monument, telling how, when, and by whom all these things were done, is itself a monument of self-satisfaction.

The city walls, with their towers at regular intervals, even yet in very good preservation, bound the Dane John grounds in one direction. Still goes a broad walk on the summit of those walls, and the pilgrim might imagine himself a sentry guarding the mediæval city, were it not that dense and sordid suburbs spread beyond, on whose blank walls soap and cheap tea advertisements alternate with others crying the virtues of infants' foods and the latest quack nostrums.

THE DANE JOHN, CANTERBURY.

Canterbury is Canterbury yet, and Becket is still its prophet, but some things be changed. Electric lighting—of a marvellously poor illuminating quality it is true, and vastly inferior to the gas they brew at the Castle, but yet electric lighting of sorts—somewhat remodernises its streets; but it is still true, as at any time since Popery came down crash, that you cannot obtain lodging without money, or miracles, whether or no. Becket, however, still pervades the place. His arms—the three black Cornish choughs, red-beaked and clawed, on a blue field—have been adopted by the city, and every shop patronised by visitors sells china or trinkets painted or engraved with them. Pictures of the transept where he fell on that day of long ago; yea, even photographs of the skull and bones discovered some years since, and thought to be his, are at every turn. Becket is not forgot, and a certain portly Tudor shade—the wraith of one who ordained all worship and reverence of him to cease and every vestige of his shrine and relics to be destroyed—must surely be furiously and impotently angered. Little need, however, for that kingly shade to be thus perturbed; this modern and local cult of Saint Thomas is only business at Canterbury—and very good business, too.

Still goes the tourist-pilgrim along the way to the Cathedral trod by the sinners of mediæval times, to purge them of their sins and start afresh. Where they turned off to the left from the main street, down Mercery Lane, the present-day visitors still turn, and the Christchurch Gate, at the end of the narrow lane, opens as of old into the Cathedral precincts. It is a wonderful gatehouse, this of Christchurch, built by Prior Goldstone nigh upon four hundred years ago, and elaborately carved with Tudor roses, portcullises, and things now so blunted by time that it is difficult to distinguish them. Time has dissolved much of the worthy Prior's noble structure, like so much sugar.

It was here, in this open space in front of the Gate, that the quaint Butter Market stood until quite recently. Tardily eager to honour one of her sons, Canterbury was so ill-advised as to sweep away the curious Butter Market to make room for the new memorial to Christopher Marlowe, the great dramatist of Shakespearean times, whose birthplace still stands in St. George's Street. It is a cynical freak of time that honour should be done to Marlowe at such a spot, for the Church in his lifetime held him to be "a wretch," a "filthy play-maker," an "atheist and a sottish swine," and it was thought that the unknown person who slew him in his thirtieth year was someone who thus revenged his insults to religion.

The Marlowe Memorial deserves attention. It is in the form of a nude bronze figure representing the Muse of Poetry, placed on a stone pedestal, and in the act of playing upon a lyre; but it is an exceedingly plump and eminently erotic, rather than intellectual, figure thus made to stand for the Muse—a Doll Tearsheet, with a coarse, sensual face, most inappropriately shaded by a wreath of poetic bays. The last touch of vulgarity is that especially municipal idea of giving the whole thing a smart finish by surrounding it with four ornate street-lamps.

THE DARK ENTRY.

Burgate Street, branching off from this point to the right, is the street where Barham was born; but our present business is to the Close, and round the south side of the Cathedral to the east end, where the Norman infirmary ruins stand. Turning here to the left, a narrow, stone-paved passage, in between high, ancient walls, leads crookedly through the romantic remains of the domestic buildings of the old monastery to the cloisters and the north side of the Cathedral. It is a twilight place, even now, in the brightest days of summer, and was once, before portions of it were unroofed, much darker. That was the time when it obtained its existing name of the "Dark Entry." If the pages of the *Ingoldsby Legends* are opened, and the legend of "Nell Cook" is read, much will be found on the subject of this gloomy passage. That legend is the "King's Scholar's Story": the terror of a schoolboy of King Henry VIII.'s school, on the north side of the precincts, at the prospect of being sent back by the haunted entry after dark, on a Friday, when the ghost of Nell Cook was supposed to have its weekly outing. Well might anyone believing in ghosts and omens especially desire not to meet that spirit, for such an encounter was supposed to presage the death of the person within the year:

THE DARK ENTRY, CANTERBURY.

"Now nay, dear Uncle Ingoldsby, now send me not I pray,
Back by that Entry dark, for that you know's the nearest way;
I dread that Entry dark with Jane alone at such an hour,
It fears me quite—it's Friday night!—and then Nell Cook hath
    pow'r."

"And who, silly child, is Nell Cook?" asks Uncle Ingoldsby; and the King's
Scholar answers:

"It was in bluff King Harry's days, while yet he went to shrift,
And long before he stamped and swore, and cut the Pope
    adrift;
There lived a portly Canon then, a sage and learned clerk;
He had, I trow, a goodly house, fast by that Entry dark.

"The Canon was a portly man—of Latin and of Greek,

And learned lore, he had good store,—yet health was on his
  cheek.
The Priory fare was scant and spare, the bread was made of
  rye,
The beer was weak, yet he was sleek—he had a merry eye.

"For though within the Priory the fare was scant and thin,
The Canon's house it stood without;—he kept good cheer
  within;
Unto the best he prest each guest, with free and jovial look,
And Ellen Bean ruled his *cuisine*.—He called her 'Nelly
  Cook.'"

It is not a very proper story that the King's Scholar unfolds; of how a "niece"
of the Canon comes to stay with him, and arouses the jealousy of the good-
looking cook, whose affections that "merry eye" of the Canon had captured.
Nell Cook thereupon successfully poisons the Canon and the strange lady
with "some nasty doctor's stuff," with which she flavours a pie destined for
the Canonical table, and the two are found as the Scholar tells:

"The Canon's head lies on the bed,—his niece lies on the
  floor!
They are as dead as any nail that is in any door!"

Nell Cook, for her crime, says Tom Ingoldsby, adapting to his literary uses the
legend long current in Canterbury, was buried alive beneath one of the great
paving-stones of the "Dark Entry"; when, local history does not inform us:

But one thing's clear—that's all the year, on every Friday
  night,
Throughout that Entry dark doth roam Nell Cook's unquiet
  sprite.

And whoever meets Nell Cook is bound to die some untimeous death within
the year! Certainly, the Dark Entry is not a place greatly frequented after
nightfall, even nowadays—but that is perhaps less by reason of superstitious
fears than because it leads to nowhere in particular.

CHAPTER IV

THE CATHEDRAL: THE MURDER OF BECKET

It is by the south porch that the Cathedral is entered. Let none suppose this to be the veritable Cathedral that Becket knew; that was replaced, piece by piece, in the succeeding centuries, all save the Norman transept where he met his fate. The nave, by whose lofty, aspiring perspective we advance, was built in 1380 upon the site of that of the twelfth century. According to the testimony of the time, it was in a ruinous condition. Conceive, if you can, the likelihood of one of those particularly massive Norman naves like those of Tewkesbury and Gloucester, which this resembled, becoming ruinous! The more probable truth of the matter is that the feeling of the time had grown inimical to those cavernous interiors of the older architects, and sought any excuse for tearing them down and building in their stead in the lightsome character of the Perpendicular period.

This nave, then, much later than Becket's era, leads somewhat unsympathetically to that most interesting spot in the whole Cathedral, the north transept. Here is the "Martyrdom," as that massive Norman cross-limb where Becket fell beneath the swords and axes of his murderers is still called. You look down into it from the steps leading into the choir and choir-aisles, as into a pit. Little changed, in the midst of all else that has been altered, this north transept alone remains very much as it was when he was slain, more than seven hundred years ago, and the sight of its stern, massive walls does much to bring back to those who behold them that fierce scene which, in the passage of all those years and the heaping of dull verbiage piled up by industrious Dryasdusts and beaters of the air, has been dulled and blunted.

Barham—our witty and mirthful Tom Ingoldsby—felt a keen personal interest in this scene, for was not his ancestor—as he conceived him to be—Reginald FitzUrse, the chief actor in that bloody scene of Becket's death? He is flippant, it must be allowed, in the reference he makes to the occurrence in the *Ingoldsby Legends*:

> A fair Cathedral, too, the story goes,
> And kings and heroes lie entombed within her;
> There pious Saints in marble pomp repose,
> Whose shrines are worn by knees of many a sinner;
> There, too, full many an aldermanic nose
> Roll'd its loud diapason after dinner;
> And there stood high the holy sconce of Becket,

—Till four assassins came from France to crack it.

Historians have not yet agreed upon the character of Becket, and no final conclusion is ever likely to be arrived at upon the vexed question of who was right and who wrong in the long-drawn contention between King and Archbishop. It is easy to shirk the point and to decide that neither was right; but another and a more just resort is to declare, after due consideration, that in the attempted secular encroachments of the Crown, and in the resistance of the Archbishop to any interference with the prerogatives and jurisdiction of the Church and the clergy, both sides were impelled by the irresistible force of circumstances. Becket was of English origin, and the first of the downtrodden Saxon race who had won to such preferment since the Norman rule began. Thus, besides being bound to defend the Church, of which he had become the head, he was regarded by the people, who idolised him, as their champion against those ruling classes whose mailed tyranny crushed them to earth.

A prime difficulty in judging the character of Becket is the extraordinary change in his conduct after he had been induced to accept the Primacy, that goal and crown of the clerical career ardently desired by all, and attained by Becket in his forty-third year. Long the favourite of the King, and already, as Chancellor, at the height of power and magnificence, there was little advantage in this elevation to the throne of Saint Augustine, and he seemed singularly unfitted to fill it, for until that juncture he had been among the most worldly of men. As Chancellor, his magnificence had outshone that of the King, he himself was gay and debonnair, clothed in purple and fine linen, feasting royally, and with hundreds of knights in his train. Nothing that the world could give had he denied himself. He was not only impressed personally with his unfitness, but the monks of Canterbury themselves, in conclave, desired to elect one of their own choice. It was, therefore, against the desire of the Church and against his own better judgment, foreseeing as he did much of the trouble that was to come, that he was given the headship.

But once enthroned, his conduct changed. He dismissed his magnificent household, feasted no more, expended his substance in charity and himself in good works; became, indeed, and in very truth, that Right Reverend Father in God which the simulacra, the windbags, the ravening wolves, the emptinesses that for hundreds of years have occupied his place, are styled. The sinner saved must be prepared for misunderstandings—it is part of the cross and burden he has taken up. The scarlet sins of the unregenerate are remembered against the saint, and his saintliness becomes to his old boon companions a hypocritical farce. That is why Becket's contemporaries did not understand him; that, too, is why so many, dimly fumbling by the rush-light glimmer of their little sputtering intelligences, presently choked and dowsed in the dusty, cobwebby garrets of incredible accretions of lies, mistakes, perversions and general rag-bag of pitiful futilities, have been left wandering in infinite darkness, and content so to wander in estimating him.

It was the sinners whose poisonous tongues did, by dint of much persistence, estrange the King's affections from Becket within a year, and their innuendoes were remembered when a growing struggle over disputed privileges found the Archbishop immovably set upon what he regarded as his duty, and not at all prepared to favour the King. If Henry had supposed the Archbishop whom he had created would be in every sense his creature, he must have been furious at his gross mistake. The fury of the Norman kings was like the unrestrained paroxysms of a raving maniac, and opposition threw them into transports of rage, felt severely by animate and inanimate objects alike. This second Henry, whose eyes were said to have in repose been gentle and dove-like, is no exception. Ill fares the messenger who brings him bad news—as ill sometimes as though he had brought about the untoward things of which he tells. Slight displeasure means a thump, a resounding smack on the face from the Royal hands, or a right Royal kick on that part where honour is so easily hurt. May not enquiring minds, diligently bent on running to earth the origin of the still existing etiquette of retreating backwards from the presence of the sovereign, find it in a natural desire of courtiers at all hazards to protect that honour?

Conceive, then, the really Royal rage of this King, bearded by someone not to be dissuaded, persuaded, admonished, or let or hindered in any particular. He became like a wild beast, tearing whatever came in his way, flinging off his clothes, throwing himself on the floor and gnawing the straw and rushes, and not merely kicking the posteriors of messengers, but flying at them with intent to tear out their eyes.

What was that which wrought such enmity between such old-time friends? Not merely one, but many things, but first and last among them the determination of the King that the clergy, instead of being amenable for offences only to the ecclesiastical courts, should be answerable to the civil tribunals. This, the earliest of the at last happily successful series of blows at clerical privilege, seemed to Becket almost sacrilegious, and he determined to protect the Church against what was, he honestly thought, according to his lights and his sacerdotal sympathies, an unwarranted attack.

By all accounts this saint was not, in his new character, the most tactful of men. With the old courtier days gone by, he had discarded the courtier-like speech, and austerely held his own. Jealous of him, several great dignitaries of the Church supported the King: among them the Archbishop of York, and the Bishops of London and Salisbury. Becket, as their spiritual chief, hurled excommunication at them, and it was even feared that he would do the same by the King. Then, in fear of his life, he went into six years' exile, ended by a pretence of reconciliation that was patently a pretence, even before he sailed for England. He was weary of exile, and ready to lay down his life for the Church.

It was early in December 1170 that he returned to Canterbury, "to die," as he prophetically had said, before embarking. Quarrels, insults, and petty persecutions met him, and thus sped December to its close. On Christmas Day he preached in the Cathedral on the text, as he read it (an all-important reservation), "On earth, peace to men of good will." "There is no peace," he declared, "but to men of good will," and with solemn meaning, readily understood by the great congregation that heard him, spoke of the martyrs who had fallen in olden days. It was possible, he added, that they would soon have another.

"Father," wailed that assembled multitude, "why do you desert us so soon? To whom will you leave us?" But, heedless of the interruption, he passed from a plaintive strain to one of fiery indignation, ending, in a voice of thunder, by a full and particular excommunication of many of his enemies and persecutors. "May they be cursed," his voice resounded through the building, "by Jesus Christ, and may their memory be blotted out of the assembly of the saints, whoever shall sow discord between me and my lord the King." So saying, he, with mediæval symbolism, dashed down a lighted candle upon the stones, to typify the extinction of those accurst, and, with religious exaltation on his face, left the pulpit, saying to his crossbearer, "One martyr, St. Alphege, you have already; another, if God will, you will have soon."

Already, while he spoke, his furrow was drawing to its end. Over in Normandy, where the King was keeping Christmas, the Archbishop of York and the Bishops of London and Salisbury were suggesting that it would be a good thing if there were no Becket. "So long as Thomas lives," said one, "you will have neither good days, nor peaceful kingdom, nor quiet life."

The thought thus instilled into the King's mind threw him into a frenzy. "A fellow," he shouted—"a fellow that has eaten my bread has lifted up his heel against me; a fellow that I loaded with benefits has dared to insult the King and the whole Royal family, and tramples on the whole kingdom; a fellow that came to Court on a lame sumpter-mule sits without hindrance on the throne itself. What sluggard wretches, what cowards, have I brought up in my Court, who care nothing for their allegiance to their master! Not one will deliver me from this low-born, turbulent priest!" So saying, he rushed from the room, doubtless to roll in one of those ungovernable Plantagenet rages upon the floor of some secluded chamber.

The four knights who from among that Court sprang forth to prove themselves, even to the awful extremities of sacrilege and murder, true King's men, were Reginald FitzUrse, Hugh de Moreville, William de Tracy, and Richard le Bret. In the light of later events, the monkish chroniclers, eager to discover the marvellous in every circumstance of the tragedy, found a dark significance in their very names. FitzUrse, they said, was of truly bear-like character; De Moreville's name proclaimed him to be of "the city of death"; Le Bret was "the brute." With so much ingenuity available, it is quite surprising they could not twist Tracy's name into something allusive to murder; but they had to be content with the weak suggestion that he was of "parricidal wickedness." All save Le Bret had been knights owning fealty to Becket while he was Chancellor.

It is detailed in these pages, in the description of Saltwood Castle, how they landed in England and made for Canterbury. A dreadful circumstance is that they knew perfectly well on whom to call when they reached the city, and waited upon a sympathiser with the King, Clarembald, the Abbot of St. Augustine's, who is thus sufficiently implicated.

From the Abbot's lodging they sent a command, ordering the Mayor to issue a proclamation in the King's name forbidding any help being given to the Archbishop. Then they took horse again and rode to the Palace, accompanied by their men-at-arms, whom they posted in a house hard by the gateway. The short day of December 29th was nearly at its close when they drew rein in the courtyard beneath the great hall of the Palace, where the Archbishop and his household had but just retired from supper. They had left their swords outside, and came as travellers, their mailed armour concealed under long cloaks. Entering the hall they met the seneschal, who ushered them into the private room where the Archbishop sat, among his intimates. "My lord," he said, "here are four knights from King Henry wishing to speak with you"; and they were bidden enter.

FitzUrse began the furious discussion. The knights had seated themselves on the floor at the Archbishop's feet, and waited until he should finish the conversation he was holding with a monk. When Becket turned and looked calmly at each in turn, ending with saluting Tracy by name, FitzUrse it was who broke in with a contemptuous "God help you!"

The Archbishop's face flushed crimson. He was a man of vehement nature, and it is wonderful that he restrained himself from striking that insolent intruder. "We have a message from the King over the water," continued FitzUrse; "tell us whether you will hear it in private, or in the hearing of all."

Within the hearing of all that message, such as it was, was given. It was but a reiteration of old demands and old grievances, made to goad the Archbishop into fury, and to afford an excuse for an attack upon him. The discussion aroused both sides to anger, and the knights, calling upon all to prevent the Archbishop from escaping, dashed off, with the cry of "To arms!" for their swords.

But Becket harboured no thoughts of escape. Although he perceived that death was near, he made no retreat, being indeed, by this time, fanatically bent upon the martyr's crown. Outside, the signal had been already given to the men-at-arms, who now came pouring in, with shouts of "Réaux!" or "King's men." The knights now returned, their swords girt about them. Already, however, the Archbishop's attendants had closed and barred the doors, and were endeavouring to save him from that death he seemed to welcome. With kindly violence they pushed and pulled him by obscure passages from the Palace and along the cloisters, while the blows of axes and the splintering of wood told how in their rear the murderers were hewing their way onward. Thus at last, strenuously resisting, he was impelled towards the door that opened from the cloisters into the north transept.

Once within the Cathedral the monks bolted the door behind them, and in their haste excluded some of their brethren, thus left, unprotected, to face the onrush of armed men. Hearing these unfortunate ones vainly knocking for admittance, Becket, exerting all his authority, commanded the door to be opened; and when he found his words disregarded, broke away from those who held him and drew back the bolts with his own hands.

Seeing the way thus made clear for those pursuing men of wrath, the crowd of anxious monks surrounding the Archbishop immediately turned and fled to those hiding-places they knew of. Only three remained, dauntless, by their chief. These were Robert of Merton, William FitzStephen, and Edward Grim, who stood by him, vainly imploring him to flee. Only one concession he made to their entreaties. He would go to the choir, and there, before the high altar, the holiest place in the Cathedral, with all dignity make an end.

It was as he was thus ascending the steps from the transept that the knights burst into the sacred building. Bewildered at first by the almost complete darkness, they could only shout at random, "Where is Thomas Becket, traitor to the King?" No answer. Then, falling over a monk, came an oath, from FitzUrse, and the question, "Where is the Archbishop?" Becket himself answered, and descending again into the transept, confronted them. He stood in front of what was then the the Chapel of St. Benedict, and calmly asked, "Reginald, why do you come into my church armed?" For answer FitzUrse thrust a carpenter's axe he had found against his breast, and with a savage oath declared, "You shall die: I will tear out your heart!" "Fly!" exclaimed another, not so eager to commit the sin of sacrilege, before which the mediæval world recoiled; "Fly! or you are a dead man!" striking him with the flat of his sword, to emphasise the warning.

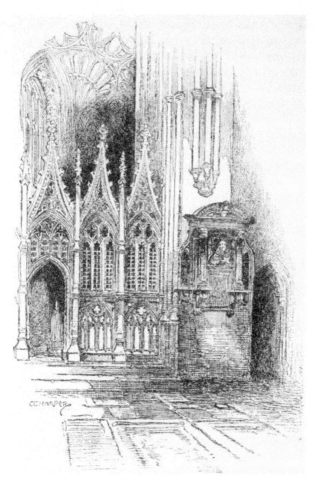

THE "MARTYRDOM," CANTERBURY CATHEDRAL.

Then the four united their efforts to drag him from the Cathedral, but without success. Himself a powerful man, he seized Tracy and flung him heavily upon the pavement. FitzUrse, advancing upon him with a drawn sword, he called by a vile name, adding, "You profligate wretch, you are my man; you have done me fealty; you ought not to touch me." No fear, it will be seen, in all this, but a not unreasonable fury, somewhat obscuring the martyr spirit. Fury on both sides, for FitzUrse, losing the last atom of restraint, and yelling "Strike!" aimed a blow with his great, two-handed sword that, had it been better directed, must have smote off the Archbishop's head. As it was, it merely skimmed off his cap. Becket, who must have been momentarily surprised to find himself still alive, then covered his eyes with his hands, and bending his head, was heard to commend his cause and the cause of the Church to God, to St. Denis of France, to St. Alphege and all the saints of the Church. Tracy then dealt a blow, partly intercepted by Grim, whose arm, protecting the Archbishop, was broken by it. By this time blood was trickling down the Archbishop's face. He wiped it away and murmured, "Into Thy hands, O Lord, I commend my spirit;" and then, falling at a further blow from Tracy, "For the name of Jesus, and for the defence of the Church, I am willing to die." There he lay, and so lying, received a tremendous stroke from Richard le Bret, who accompanied it with the exclamation, "Take this, for love of my lord William, brother of the King!" That stroke not only clove away the upper part of the skull, but the sword itself was broken in two. Vengeance was accomplished.

When the assassins fled from that scene of blood, it was quite dark. They went as they had come, by the cloisters, shouting that they were "King's men," and cursing and stumbling over unfamiliar steps. A servant of the Archdeacon of Sens was sufficiently unfortunate to be wailing for the cruel death of the Archbishop when they passed, and foolish enough to be in their way. They fell over him, and, still heady with that struggle and the lust of blood, gave him in passing a mailed kick, and so tremendous a sword-thrust that for long afterwards he had sufficient occasion to lament for himself.

It was something of an anti-climax to their murderous passions that they should, as they now did, repair to the Archbishop's Palace and make a burglarious raid upon the gold and silver vessels of the church, and loot from Becket's stables the magnificent horses he kept. With this personal plunder, and with a mass of the Archbishop's documents and papers seized on behalf of the King, they were preparing to depart when the very unusual circumstance in December of a violent thunderstorm set a final scene of horror upon that closing day.

The news fell heavily upon the people of Canterbury, who reverenced Becket far more than did those within the Church who had immediately surrounded him; and the citizens came rushing like an irresistible torrent into the Cathedral as soon as they heard of the sacrilegious deed.

Like the greater number of our cathedrals, this of Canterbury has been greatly altered since that time. It was into a Norman nave that the excited populace thronged—a building that must have closely resembled the still-existing nave of that period at Gloucester, gloomy and dark at the best of times, but on this December evening a well of infinite blackness, faintly illuminated by the distant lights twinkling in the choir and on the high altar. This horror-stricken crowd was only with great difficulty forced back and at last shut out, and it was long before the monks returned to the transept where the Archbishop had fallen before the blows of the four. There his body lay in the dark, as it had been left, his blood still wet on those cold stones, as Osbert, the chamberlain, entering with a single light, held out at arm's length in that cavern of blackness and unimaginable gloom, steps in it, and, if he be not quite different from other men, shudders and almost drops his glimmering candle when he finds what awful moisture that is in which he has been walking. Osbert alone has ventured to seek his master. Where, then, are the others of his household? In hiding, like those monks who, now that all is still, venture, like rats, to come from their hiding-holes in chapel and triforium, or from secret places contrived for such emergencies in the roof.

The Archbishop lay upon his face, the upper part of his scalp sliced off by that whirling blow of Tracy's, and the contents of his head spilled over the pavement, just as a bowl of liquid might be overset. Osbert, with rare fortitude, replaces that scalp as one might replace a lid, and binding the head, he and the monks between them place the body upon a bier and carry it to the high altar in the choir.

There were those among the monks who felt small sympathy for Becket. To them he was but a proud worldling whose remarkable preferment to the Primacy had been scandalous, and whose quarrels with the King had been, they thought, dictated more for the advancement of his own personal authority than for sake of a purely impersonal desire to preserve and cherish the rights of the Church. He had been elected Archbishop by desire of the King and against the feeling of the Priory, and they thought he should, in consequence, have been more complaisant to Royal demands. They were not a little jealous of the man set to rule over them, and moreover, could not at once perceive the martyr and the saint in the dignitary thus at last struck down in that long struggle. They were horror-stricken at the sacrilege of it, but did not burst into grief and lamentations for the individual until that happened which put a very different complexion upon the dead Archbishop's character. Far into the night, as the monks sat in the choir around that silent figure, his aged friend and instructor, Robert of Merton, told them of the secret austerities of his later life, and made a revelation that wholly changed their mental attitude. To prove his words, he exposed the many layers of the clothing to those who gathered round, and showed how, beneath all, and next the skin, the "luxurious" Archbishop had worn the habit of a monk, and had endured the disciplinary discomfort of a hair-shirt. There, too, on the skin, were visible the weals of the daily scourgings by which the Archbishop mortified the flesh. Nor was this the sum of his virtues, for when, a little later, his garments were removed, previous to interment, they were found to be swarming with vermin; that hair-cloth, itself so penitential, densely populated with a crawling mass whose presence must have made it more penitential still.

According to the accounts of those who beheld these transcendent proofs of sanctity, the hair-cloth was bubbling over with these inhabitants, like water in a simmering cauldron.

At sight of such unmistakable evidences of holiness the brethren went into hysterics. "See, see," they said to one another, "what a true monk he was, and we knew it not!"—an oblique and unpleasing reflection upon the personal habits of the monastic orders. They kissed him, as he lay dead there, and called him "St. Thomas," and at last, unwilling that any tittle of his sanctity should be impugned, buried him in his verminous condition.

Meanwhile, newly alive to the saintly character of him whom they now clearly perceived to be a martyr, orders were given to rail off the spot where he had fallen, and for every trace of his blood to be jealously preserved. But unhappily for the Church, the common people, who had from the moment of his death regarded their Archbishop as a martyred saint, had already soaked up the greater part of that precious blood in strips hastily torn from their clothes, and had been given his stained and splashed outer garments. These were losses that could never be made good, but they did not greatly matter to those who could so dilute the little remaining blood that it sufficed to supply the uncounted thousands of pilgrims who made pilgrimage to the shrine of St. Thomas for the space of three hundred and fifty years, and took away with them little phials containing, as they fondly believed, so intimate a relic of England's most powerful saint.

In spite of the dark legends that tell how vengeance overtook the assassins, it does not seem to be the fact that they were adequately punished for their fearful crime, and certainly no Royal displeasure lighted upon them. "The wicked," we are told, "flee when no man pursueth," and the knights, fearful of the revenge that might be taken upon them by the people of Canterbury, rode off, unhindered, with their small escort of men-at-arms, to Saltwood. Within that stronghold they felt safe. That they would have been equally safe at Canterbury we may suppose, for Robert de Broc, shut up within the strong walls of the Archbishop's Palace, felt strong enough to threaten the monks with what he would do if they dared so honour the dead Prelate as to bury him among the tombs of the Archbishops. He would, he declared, tear out the body, hang it from a gibbet, hew it in pieces, and throw the fragments by the highway, to be devoured by swine or birds of prey. It is quite evident that Robert de Broc was a good hater and a very thorough partisan of the King. The monks did well to be afraid of him, and meekly forbearing from giving offence, laid their martyr in the crypt.

The four lay only one night at Saltwood. The next day they rode to the old manor-house of South Malling, near Lewes, itself a property belonging to the

Archbishops, and throwing down their arms and accoutrements upon a dining-table in the hall, gathered comfortably round the cheerful hearth, when —says the legend—the table, unwilling to bear that sacrilegious burden, started back and threw the repugnant load on the ground. The arms were replaced by the startled servants, who came rushing in with torches; but again they were flung away, this time with even greater force. It was one of the knights who, with blanched face, declared the supernatural nature of this happening.

The following morning they were off again, bound for Hugh de Moreville's far distant Yorkshire castle of Knaresborough, where they remained for one year. It would have been too scandalous a thing for the King to receive his bravos at once, for he had a part of his own to play that would have been quite spoiled by such indecent haste—a dramatic part, but one that fails to carry any conviction of its sincerity. It was at Argenton that he heard of the successful issue of his commission, and on receipt of the news isolated himself for three days, refused all food but milk of almonds, rolled himself in penitential sackcloth and ashes, and grievously called upon God to witness that he was not responsible for the Archbishop's death. "Alas!" exclaimed that trembling hypocrite, "alas! that it ever happened."

But it is not in empty lamentations, real or feigned, that penitence is found. The assassins went unpunished, and, together with others of Becket's bitterest enemies within and without the Church, were even promoted. Before two years had passed the four knights were found constantly at the King's Court, on familiar terms with him and his companions in hunting. It is a cynical commentary upon the kingly penitence that one of the murderers, William de Tracy, became Justiciary of Normandy. But something had to be done to expiate a deed whose echoes rumbled horrifically throughout Europe. The Pope, Alexander III., indicated a course of fighting against the infidel in the Holy Land, and it seems probable that they did so work off their sins; all except Tracy, who, having made over his Devonshire manor of Daccombe to the Church, for the maintenance of a monk for ever, to celebrate masses for the repose of the souls of the living and the dead, set out for Palestine, but was for so long driven back by contrary winds that he almost despaired of setting foot abroad. This especial retribution meted out to him was for the particular heinousness of having dealt the first effective blow at the martyr. When at last he was carried to the coast of Calabria, he was seized with a mysterious disease at Cosenza, a disease whose agonies made him tear the flesh from his bones with his own hands. Thus entreating, "Mercy, St. Thomas!" he perished miserably.

The mysticism of the time told many dreadful legends. Dogs refused to eat from the tables of the murderers; grass would not grow where their feet went; those they loved were doomed to misery and death.

From the King a certain humiliation was demanded, but it amounted to little beyond an oath, taken on the gospels before the Papal legates, that he had not ordered or desired the murder, and an expressed readiness to restore property belonging to the See of Canterbury. This easy satisfaction was given at Avranches, in May 1172, but if it was sufficient for the Pope it did by no means calm the English people, who saw in the cumulative domestic troubles and foreign disasters of the time the wrath of Heaven. The greater penance of 1174 was accordingly decided upon. Arriving from Normandy on July 8th, he journeyed to Canterbury, to the shrine of the already sainted martyr, by the Pilgrims' Road, living the while upon bread and water. Coming to Harbledown, he resigned horseback for a barefooted walk into the city. Thus, with a mere woollen shirt and a cloak, he came to the Cathedral, kneeling in the porch, and then proceeding directly to the scene of the martyrdom, where he again knelt and kissed the stone where the Archbishop had died. From that spot, he was conducted to the crypt, where the tomb still remained, and, placing his head and shoulders in the tomb itself, received on his shoulders five strokes of a rod from each bishop and abbot present, and three each from the by-standing eighty monks. This discipline must have killed him had those monks laid on with the hearty goodwill customary with prison warders; but their stripes were mere formalities, and the King departed the next morning, after passing a solitary fasting vigil in the crypt, where, during the solemn hours of the night, he had had ample opportunity of repentance. From Canterbury he rode to London, absolved and with a whole skin.

The nation saw much virtue in this public reparation. How could they fail so to do when the affairs of the realm took an immediate and decided turn for the better, when the King of Scots, long a terror in the north, was captured at Alnwick, and when the invading fleet of Henry's own rebellious son was repulsed? The forgiveness and the miraculous intercession of the beatified Thomas were prompt and efficacious.

The cult of this peculiarly sainted person was extraordinary, and far transcended that of any other martyr. To his shrine, erected in a place of especial honour, and encrusted with gold and gems, the pilgrims of many nations and many centuries flocked, greatly to the enrichment of the Church. The miraculous cures wrought at his tomb, and the marvellous legends that clustered around the story of his life and death, were the theme of ages. But the gross superstitions, and the grosser scandals, tricks, and miscellaneous knaveries that were encouraged by that martyr-worship had discredited him by the time of Henry VIII., that less superstitious age when it was possible for the King and his advisers to declare "Thomas Becket" a traitor, to submit his relics to every indignity, to destroy them and his shrine, and to seize all the endowments and valuables connected with his worship.

The great destruction wrought at the Reformation accounts for the scantiness of Becket's memorials. Here, in the "Martyrdom," only the Norman walls that looked down upon the scene, and some portions of the pavement, are left. A square piece of stone, inserted in the middle of a large slab, marks the exact spot where he fell, and tells how the original stone, regarded as of a peculiar sanctity, had been at some time or another removed.

CHAPTER V

TAPPINGTON HALL

The central point of the Ingoldsby Country is, of course, the Ingoldsby manor house of Tappington Hall. To discover this we must leave Canterbury by the Dover Road, and, climbing up to the rise of Gutteridge Gate, where a gibbet stood in ancient times and a turnpike-gate until recent years, drop down into the village of Bridge, whose name derives from an arch thrown at an early period across the River Stour. At the summit of the corresponding rise out of Bridge, the road, running exactly on the site of the Roman Watling Street, comes to that bleak and elevated table-land known as Barham Downs, the scene of Cæsar's great battle with the Britons on July 23rd, A.D. 56. Twenty-seven thousand Roman soldiers, horse and foot, met the wild rush of the Britons, who, with the usual undisciplined and untaught courage of uncivilised races, flung themselves upon the invaders and were thrown back by the impenetrable wall of the serried phalanxes. Recoiling dismayed from this reception, they were instantly pursued by the Roman cavalry and cut up into isolated bands, who fought courageously all that fatal day in the dense woodlands. Protected by mounds and trenches defended with palisades of stakes cunningly interwoven with brushwood, they prolonged the hopeless contest until nightfall, and then fell back. Cæsar, describing these woodland forts as *oppida*, gives especial attention to one particularly troublesome stronghold. "Being repulsed," he writes, "they withdrew themselves into the woods and reached a place which they had prepared before, having closed all approaches to it by felled timber." This retreat was captured by the soldiers of the Seventh Legion, who, throwing up a mound against it, advanced, holding their shields over their heads in the military formation known as "the tortoise," and drove out the defenders at the sword's point.

This, the last place to hold out, is, despite the eighteen and a half centuries that have passed, still to be seen in Bourne Park, on the summit of Bridge Hill, and is familiarly known in the neighbourhood as "Old England's Hole." "Never forget," the old countryfolk have been wont to impress their children —"never forget that this is Old England's Hole, and that on this spot a last stand for freedom was made by your British forefathers."

Everyone in the neighbourhood knows Old England's Hole. It is seen beside the road, on the right hand, just where the cutting through the crest of the hill, made in 1829, to ease the pull-up for the coach-horses, begins. At that same time the course of the road was very slightly diverted, and, instead of actually impinging upon this ancient historic landmark, as before, was made to run a few feet away. Now the spot is seen across the fence of the park, the old course of the road still traceable beside it, as a slightly depressed grassy track,

plentifully dotted with thistles. The stronghold consists of a crater-like hollow, encircled by earthen banks, still high and steep. A great number of ash-trees and thorns, some very old, gnarled, and decayed, grow on these banks, and cast a dense shade upon the interior.

THE VALE OF BARHAM.

Barham Downs, stretching for three miles, windswept and bare, above the valley of the Lesser Stour, form a tract of country that must needs appeal strongly to the imaginative man. Only the bunkers and other recent impudent interferences of some local golf club have ever disturbed the ancient lines of Roman entrenchments.

Barham Downs are, of course, the "Tappington Moor," of that terrible legend, the "Hand of Glory," which opens the collection of the *Ingoldsby Legends* in many editions:

> On the lone bleak moor, At the midnight hour,
> Beneath the Gallows Tree,
> Hand in hand The Murderers stand,
> By one, by two, by three!
> And the Moon that night With a grey, cold light,
> Each baleful object tips;
> One half of her form Is seen through the storm,
> The other half's hid in Eclipse!
> And the cold Wind howls, And the Thunder growls,
> And the Lightning is broad and bright;
> And altogether It's very bad weather,
> And an unpleasant sort of a night!

Barham village, a very different place, lies below, snugly embosomed amid the rich trees of the Stour valley, sheltered and warm. From this point its tall, tapering, shingled spire peeps out from among the massed trees, and a branch

road leads directly

down to it and to that park and mansion of Barham Court which, had his ancestors of remote times done their duty by posterity, the author of the *Ingoldsby Legends* firmly believed would have been his.

THE "EAGLE GATES," BROOME PARK.

But here we are come, on the high road, to a striking entrance to a park. The place seems strangely familiar, yet the "Eagle Gates," as the countryfolk call them, of this domain of Broome Park are certainly unknown to us. The mystery is only explained by referring to the woodcut which prefaces most editions of the *Ingoldsby Legends*, and purports to be a view of "Tappington, taken from the Folkestone Road." Then it is seen that the illustration rather closely resembles this spot, with the trifling exceptions that eagles, and not lions, surmount the pillars, and that the mansion of Broome is really not to be seen through the gateway, although clearly visible a few yards away, when it is seen to be not unlike the house pictured. Many have been the perplexed pilgrims who have vainly sought the ancestral Ingoldsby gates and chimneys between Canterbury and Folkestone, lured to the quest by the original Preface to the *Legends*. Broome Park, whose lovely demesne is criss-crossed by turfy paths and tracks freely open to the explorer, is beautifully undulating and thickly wooded. In its midst stands the mansion, built in the last years of the seventeenth century by one of the extinct Dixwell family, and gabled, chimneyed, and generally as picturesque as Barham "most pseudonymously" described it, under the title of "Tappington Hall."

BROOME PARK: THE REAL ORIGINAL OF TAPPINGTON HALL.

The Oxenden family have long owned the beautiful old place, which still contains a "powdering closet," as used in the bygone days of huge headdresses and powdered hair. My lady would sit in her boudoir with her head thrust through a hatch in the wall into the "powdering closet"—a contrivance necessary to prevent the powder being scattered over everything.

TAPPINGTON, FROM THE FOLKESTONE ROAD.

49

Here, by the "Eagle Gates," the road branches, the left-hand route continuing to Dover, the right-hand to Folkestone. This is the "beautiful green lane" of the Preface to the *Legends*. "Here," says that Preface, addressed to the incredulous who did not believe in the existence of Tappington Hall—"here a beautiful green lane, diverging abruptly to the right, will carry them through the Oxenden plantations and the unpretending village of Denton, to the foot of a very respectable hill—as hills go in this part of Europe. On reaching its summit, let them look straight before them—and if, among the hanging woods which crown the opposite side of the valley, they cannot distinguish an antiquated manor house of Elizabethan architecture, with its gable ends, stone stanchions, and tortuous chimneys rising above the surrounding trees, why, the sooner they procure a pair of Dollond's patent spectacles the better. If, on the contrary, they can manage to descry it, and, proceeding some five or six furlongs through the avenue, will ring at the Lodgegate—they cannot mistake the stone lion with the Ingoldsby escutcheon (Ermine, a saltire engrained Gules) in his paws—they will be received with a hearty old English welcome."

DENTON.

Let us, then, proceed along the Folkestone Road, with the Oxenden plantations—now grown into dense woods of larch and pine—on the right. Wayfarers are scarce, and the lovely scenery of Broome Park and the road into Denton is quite solitary. A ladder-stile leaps the rustic fence, birds chatter and quarrel in the trees, but as you come into the hamlet of Denton, it is, in its quaint old-world appearance and apparent emptiness, like some stage scene with the actors called off. Denton is a triangular strip of village green, surrounded by picturesque cottages, and with the old sign of the "Red Lion" inn planted romantically in the centre. Beyond it comes Denton Court, screened from the road by its timbered park, with Denton Chapel close by. Of this you may read in the *Legends*; but those who, relying too implicitly upon Barham's statements, seek the brass of the Lady Rohesia, with the inscription —

" Praie for ye sowle of ye Lady Rohse,
And for alle Christen sowles "

will be doomed to disappointment, for it is one of his picturesque embellishments upon fact.

Denton Chapel is a building of the smallest dimensions, belonging to the Early English and later periods, but not distinguished by many mouldings or other features by which the date of a building is most readily to be fixed. It consists only of a nave and a plain tower; but on the north wall, beside the pulpit, there is a sculptured stone which may arouse the curiosity of the passing architect. It is probably a dedication cross, but the incised letters upon it have hitherto baffled elucidation.

More amusing, perhaps, is the colony of white owls which haunt the chapel, and from their perch on the beams above the chancel deposit upon the altar unmistakable evidence of their visits.

And now we come to Tappington. The valley opens wide, and on either side of it climb gently-rising hills clothed with thin woods, the Folkestone Road ascending the shoulder of the hills to the left. From it we look down upon a beautiful flat expanse of meadow-land; but no lodge-gate, no stone lions, no avenue, and certainly not the slightest trace of a park nor of a grand manor house can be seen. Only an old farmstead, half-smothered in ivy and creepers, is seen, in midst of the open meadow. It is a dream of rustic beauty, but—it is not the manor house of Barham's vivid fancy and picturesque pen. If, however, the rich details with which he clothed the old farm buildings of

Tappington are lacking, it yet remains of absorbing interest, quite apart from the literary memories it embodies. The old house, and the remains of a former grandeur still visible in the half-obliterated foundations of demolished buildings, attract attention. There it stands, a squat building of mellowed red brick, crossed and recrossed with timbering. Its rust-red roof is bowed and bent, and, in place of the clustered chimneys of fiction, one short and stout chimney springs from the centre of the roof-ridge, while another crowns the gable-end. In the meadow are traces of an old well which, before the greater part of Tappington Manor House was, at some unknown period, pulled down, stood in a quadrangle formed by a great range of buildings. Creepers and ivy clothe the front of the old house, and a garden,

full of all manner of old-fashioned flowers, extends on either side of the entrance.

TAPPINGTON HALL.

The interior is of more interest than might be supposed from a glance at the outside. A magnificent old carved-oak staircase conducts upstairs from the lower rooms, and on the walls hang portraits—old portraits indeed, but quite fictitiously said to be Ingoldsbys, and in fact derived by some later owner of the property from Wardour Street, or other such ready source, where not merely Ingoldsbys, but ancestors of every kind, are procurable on demand. One, with an armorial shield and the name of "Stephen Ingoldsby" painted on it, glowers sourly from the topmost stair, where the blood-stained flooring still bears witness to an extraordinary fratricide committed here two hundred and fifty years ago.

THE "MERCHANT'S-MARK" OF THOMAS MARSH OF MARSTON.

It is quite remarkable that, while Barham invented and transmuted legends that had Tappington for their centre, he never alluded to this genuine tragedy. It seems, then, that when all England was divided between the partisans of King and Commons, and Charles and his Parliament were turning families one against the other, Tappington Manor House was inhabited by two brothers, descendants of that "Thomas Marsh of Marston" who is the hero of that prose legend, "The Leech of Folkestone," and whose merchant's-mark is still to be seen here, carved on the newel of the great staircase. These two brothers had taken different sides in the struggle then going on, and quarrelled so bitterly that they agreed never to speak to one another, living actually in different parts of the then much larger house, and only using this staircase in common as they retired to or descended from their particular apartments.

TAPPINGTON HALL: NIGHT.

One night, by evil chance, they met upon the stairs. None knew what passed between them, or whether black looks or bitter words were exchanged; but as the Cavalier passed, his Puritan brother drew a dagger and stabbed him in the back. He fell, and died on the spot, and the stains of his blood are there to this day—visible, indubitably, to one's own physical eyes.

53

The good people—farming folks from Westmoreland—who lately occupied the house, showed the stranger these stains, outside what is known as the bedroom of "Bad Sir Giles," who, to quote "The Spectre of Tappington," "had been a former proprietor in the days of Elizabeth. Many a dark and dismal tradition is yet extant of the licentiousness of his life and the enormity of his offences. The Glen, which the keeper's daughter was seen to enter, but never known to quit, still frowns darkly as of yore; while an ineradicable blood-stain on the oaken stair yet bids defiance to the united energies of soap and sand. But it is with one particular apartment that a deed of more especial atrocity is said to be connected. A stranger guest—so runs the legend—arrived unexpectedly at the mansion of the 'Bad Sir Giles.' They met in apparent friendship; but the ill-concealed scowl on their master's brow told the domestics that the visit was not a welcome one." Next morning, the stranger was found dead in his bed, with marks of violence on his body. He was buried in Denton churchyard, on the other side of the highway to Folkestone. For the rest of the tale, and how the spectre was supposed to have purloined Lieutenant Seaforth's breeches, the *Ingoldsby Legends* themselves must be consulted.

Tappington has again passed away from the Barhams. Ingoldsby's son, the Reverend Richard Harris Dalton Barham, Vicar of Lolworth, Cambridgeshire, resigned that living in 1876, and retired to Dawlish, South Devon, where he died in 1886; but considerably earlier than that date he had agreed, having no children, to sell the property and divide the proceeds with his two sisters. This was accordingly done.

Although the scenery is so sweetly beautiful, the soil is said to be very poor—mostly unfertile red earth, mixed with great quantities of flints, the rest chalk. A great extent of the property is still coppice and scrubwood. An advertisement of 1890, offering the place to be let, is interesting:

FARM.—KENT.—Tappington Everard, Denton, near Canterbury, comprising Homestead, with Picturesque Residence (formerly occupied by the Rev. R. H. Barham, author of the *Ingoldsby Legends*) and about 245 Acres of Land, of which 144 Acres are Pasture, and 101 Acres Arable. Rent £220. Early possession may be had.—For terms and further particulars apply to Messrs. Worsfold & Hayward, Land Agents, Dover, and 80, Cannon Street, London, E.C.

CHAPTER VI

ROMNEY MARSH

The scene now changes to Romney Marsh. It was in 1817, in his twenty-ninth year, that Barham came to this recondite region, the Archbishop of Canterbury having collated him to the rectory of Snargate, with which went at that time, by some mysterious ecclesiastical jugglery that does not concern us, the curacy of the parish of Warehorne. He lived by preference there, rather than in the malarious marsh itself, at Snargate, and thus the vicarage house that stands, amid a recent melancholy plantation of larches, to the left of the road on entering the village, has its interest, for we may suppose that in it he lived, although, to be sure, it has undergone alterations, and its stuccoed abominations and feeble attempts at Gothic design must be later than his day. It is a disappointing house to the literary pilgrim who loves his Barham— gaunt and dismal-looking as you pass it; but the site is interesting, for we must by no means forget that it was here, driven to it by the weariness of being confined to the house after breaking his leg in a gig accident, in 1819, that he turned to literary composition. A novel called *Baldwin* was the result. It was published anonymously, and was not—nor, as a perusal of it satisfies one, did it deserve to be—a success. He was only serving his apprenticeship to letters, and had not yet discovered himself. That he speedily improved upon this first effort becomes evident in his succeeding work, begun immediately after the completion of the first. This, partly written here, was the novel of *My Cousin Nicholas*, a work of splendid and rollicking humour now undeservedly forgotten. Before he had finished the manuscript a change came over his professional prospects, for in 1821 he was induced to apply for a minor canonry of St. Paul's Cathedral, and when, to his surprise, he was elected, removed to London, and neither Warehorne nor Snargate knew him any more. Those who make this pilgrimage will think his unbounded joy at leaving his country cure perhaps a little indecent:

> Oh, I'll be off! I will, by Jove!
>   No more by purling streams I'll ramble,
> Through dirty lanes no longer rove,
>   Bemired, and scratched by briar and bramble.

He was eager for London, and preferment.

As for Warehorne itself, it is one of those smallest of villages with the biggest of churches which give the stranger the alternatives of supposing either that it has decayed from some former prosperity or that the piety of whoever built the big church outran his discretion. Perhaps he who originally built it was a sinner of more than usual calibre, the magnitude of whose misdeeds is thus feebly reflected to after ages in this architectural expiation. It is a thought of one's very own, but essentially Barhamesque

—so imbued with the spirit of the master does the pilgrim become. But at any rate, if the original portions of the church be Norman and Early English, the great heavy tower of dull red brick is commonplace eighteenth century, and owes nothing to ideas of vicarious atonement, which were not prevalent at the time of its building. "Commonplace" I have called it, and so indeed it is, and unimaginative to boot, but that is not to deny the impressiveness it gives the view. It has quite the right tone for the grim place, overhanging the mist-laden, sad-faced marsh, and the trees that have grown up around it have in some freakish sympathetic mood grown in quite the proper dramatic way. There they slant across the sky, the sweeping poplars; there between them you can glimpse the churchyard yews; and there, I doubt not, the least imaginative can picture the smugglers of Romney Marsh topping the rise, each one with a couple of brandy-tubs across his shoulders. Nay, to go further—a mental excursion for which we have due warranty in the authentic published records of Barham's own residence here—we may perceive the rector of Snargate coming home o' nights to wife and children at Warehorne rectory, and meeting on the way, in the dark, those self-same free-traders. "Stand!" they cry; and then, with relief, "It's only parson! Good-night t'ye, sir!" Had it been someone else, say a preventive man, they would have knocked him senseless to the ground, as the mildest measure they could afford.

Here, down a curving and suddenly descending road, we came unexpectedly to a railway and its closed level-crossing gates, a surprising encounter in these wilds. It is the Ashford to Rye branch of the South-Eastern—or more grandiloquently, since its alliance with the London, Chatham and Dover, the "Great Southern" Railway: great, they say, in nothing but its charges and delays.

Warehorne, to the backward view from the foot of this descent, looks another place—its church, seen to be really on a height—surrounded by apple orchards.

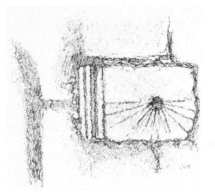

A SUNDIAL, WAREHORNE CHURCH.

No sooner is the level crossing passed than we are come to a bridge spanning a broad waterway running right and left. This marks our advent upon Romney Marsh, for here is the famous Royal Military Canal, a national defence that has never been called on to prove its usefulness, and has ever been, since its projection and execution in 1805, the subject of much satire at the expense of the military engineers who designed and constructed, and the Government that authorised it.

The origin of the canal is found in the naturally open condition of this coast, and in the old fears of invasion, not so long since dead; for there are still those who vividly recollect such alarms even in the reign of Napoleon III.

WAREHORNE.

The long range of the south coast between Eastbourne and Folkestone—a stretch of, roughly, fifty miles—is remarkable for the low sandy or shingly shores that offer easy landing for boats. The smugglers, during many centuries, found the beaches of Dymchurch, the marshes of Winchelsea, Rye, and Romney, places exactly fitted to the needs of their shy midnight business, and it has always been seen that the landing of a foreign foe could most readily be effected by an invading force on these low sand spits and shingly promontories—assuming the simultaneous absence of our fleet and the presence of a dead calm. Lying directly opposite France, whose coast can, under favourable conditions, be seen, now like a grey cloud, and again, when sunshine strikes the distant cliffs, gleaming white, the unprotected state of the Kent and Sussex littoral has always occasioned much uneasiness in times of war or rumours of war. It has never been forgotten that Cæsar landed at Deal, or that William the Norman came ashore at Pevensey, and those hoary historical lessons have served to afflict many statesmen with nightmares, away from the time when Henry VIII., in 1539, built his squat castles and potbellied bastions at Sandown, Deal, Sandgate, and Walmer, in fear of a Continental combination against him, and personally saw that they were well and truly built; down to the years of Napoleon's threatened descent, when the Military Canal was dug and the long line of Martello towers built. What says Ingoldsby of the canal? Why, this:

"When the late Mr. Pitt was determined to keep out Buonaparte and prevent his gaining a settlement in the county of Kent, among other ingenious devices adopted for that purpose he caused to be constructed what was then, and has ever since been conventionally termed, a 'Military Canal.' This is a not very practicable ditch, some thirty feet wide and nearly nine feet deep in the middle, extending from the town and port of Hythe to within a mile of the town and port of Rye, a distance of about twenty miles, and forming, as it were, the end of a bow, the arc of which constitutes that remote fifth quarter of the globe, Romney Marsh, spoken of by travellers. Trivial objections to the plan were made at the time by cavillers; an old gentleman of the neighbourhood, who proposed, as a cheap substitute, to put down his own cocked-hat upon a pole, was deservedly pooh-pooh'd down; in fact, the job, though rather an expensive one, was found to answer remarkably well. The French managed, indeed, to scramble over the Rhine and the Rhone, and other insignificant currents; but they never did, or could, pass Mr. Pitt's 'Military Canal.'"

THE ROYAL MILITARY CANAL, AT WAREHORNE.

Satire is writ large, in a fine bold Roman hand, over that description of the Military Canal, is it not? and really, the difficulty of outflanking, or even of overpassing, this insignificant waterway would have been small had Napoleon ever set forth from Boulogne. But he never did, and so its defensible properties remain only x. One thing it does do most thoroughly: being dug at the foot of the ground falling to the levels, it sets visible limits and bounds to the marshland, and in a striking manner makes you understand that here you are come into another and strange region. From Hythe, under those earthy clifflets it goes by way of Lympne, Hurst, Bonnington, Bilsington, Ruckinge, Warehorne, and Appledore, and thence to within hail of Rye, and is nowadays a most picturesque object. The word "canal" does by no means accord it justice. You picture a straight-cut stretch of water, yellow and malodorous, with barges slowly voyaging along, the bargees smoking rank shag and indulging in ranker language; but that is quite unlike this defence of Old England. It is not straight, its waters are clean, there are not any barges; but there are overhanging trees, clusters of bulrushes, strange water-plants, and an abundance of wild life along its solitary way. Before railways were, and when even the few roads of the marsh were almost impassable, the canal was very useful to the inhabitants of the district, when goods came and went along it by packet-boats; but they have long since ceased to ply. So long since as 1867 it was proposed to sell this obsolete defence to a projected railway company, but it escaped that fate.

They are chiefly beech-trees that line the banks, generally on the inner side, where the heavy raised earthworks and the corresponding ditch for defenders are still very prominent.

We are introduced to the Marshland at the beginning of the prose legend, "The Leech of Folkestone." "The world," we are told, "according to the best geographers, is divided into Europe, Asia, Africa, America, and Romney Marsh. In this last named, and fifth, quarter of the globe, a Witch may still be occasionally discovered in favourable, *i.e.* stormy, seasons, weathering Dungeness Point in an eggshell, or careering on her broomstick over Dymchurch Wall. A cow may yet be sometimes seen galloping like mad, with tail erect, and an old pair of breeches on her horns, an unerring guide to the door of the crone whose magic arts have drained her udder."

This "recondite region," as he very happily calls it, is still, sixty years after the description was written, a peculiar and eerie tract. Among the most readily defined of districts, Romney Marsh proper extends from Hythe on the east, along the coast to New Romney, in a south-westerly direction, and is bounded by the high-road between that town and Snargate on the north-west; the circuit being completed by the line of the Royal Military Canal. Other marshes, indistinguishable by the eye from that of Romney, extend westward and up to and beyond Rye and the river Rother, across the border from Kent into Sussex. These are, severally, Dunge Marsh, Walling Marsh, and Guildford Level.

Romney Marsh obtains its name from the Anglo-Saxon *Ruimn-ea*, the marshy water—the same root-word which gave Ramsgate its original name of *Ruim's-geat*. We do not know by what name the Romans knew the district; but it is quite certain that when they came to Britain, and for two centuries later, the area now covered with pastures and scattered hamlets was a great lagoon, fed by the rivers Rother and Limen and the many landsprings that even in these comparatively arid times gush from the ragged edge of the high ground between Hythe and Warehorne. With every flood tide, the sea mixed its salt waters with the fresh brought down by the rivers, which at the ebb flowed out into the sea at a point where, now nearly four miles inland, the tiny village of Old Romney is seen, standing on its almost imperceptible hillock. The Rother, now a very insignificant stream, was diverted from its old course by the terrible storm of 1280, and now seeks the sea at Rye, and the Limen has long been a mere brook; but when the Romans established themselves here, those river-channels were broad enough and deep enough to afford safe passage for the vessels of that time, and the anchorage within the great shingle-bank that then protected the lagoon from where Hythe now stands to New Romney was by far the best and safest on this coast. It is difficult at first to fully grasp these great changes that have so altered the appearance of this great tract of country within the historic period; but, once understood, they make a fascinating study and give the marsh a deeper interest. Then only is it possible to reconstruct the forgotten scene: the calm waters of the magnificent harbour stretching away for miles, to the densely wooded slopes of Ruckinge, Bonnington, and Hurst, where the oaks and the brushwood were mirrored in the shallow reaches, and the clustered vessels could be seen anchored in the fairway.

At the remotest end of this lake, where Lympne and Studfall Castle are now, were the harbour and fortress of Portus Lemanis, taking their name from the river Limen, and forming perhaps the chief commercial port of that time, just as Rutupium and Regulbium were the military and naval stations. From that point ran a road, straight as though measured by a ruler, fourteen miles inland, across country, to the Roman station and town of Durovernum: the lonely road now marked on the map as "Stone Street"; the station that city we now know as Canterbury.

At some late period in the Roman domination this magnificent harbour was found to be silting up. Many things have changed since those remote days, but the prevailing winds and the general set of the sea-currents in the Channel remain unaltered. Even then the westerly gales and the march of the shingle from west to east were altering the geography of this coast, just as they are active in doing now, adding as they do in every year great deposits of shingle to that projecting beak of Dungeness which was not in existence in the Roman era.

The consternation of the merchants and the shipping interest of Portus Lemanis at this gradual silting up of the harbour must have been great, but we know nothing of it, nor of the measures that must needs have been taken to prevent it. Probably it was the clearing of the wooded inland country that caused these changes, quite as much as the set of the shingle; for it was the dense woods that gave the Rother and the Limen their once robust existence, and when they were cut down and the moisture they generated was lost, those rivers would lose that strength of current necessary to scour away the shingly bars that began to accumulate in the estuaries. The mischief was, of course, long in the doing, and probably two hundred years passed before it was seen that the harbour and the port were doomed.

When that fact became at last impressed upon the Romans, they altered their policy. Ceasing any attempt they had made to keep the waterway open, they allied their efforts to the forces of nature, and, building walls to keep the sea out and the rivers within their courses, began that sustained work which has at last, after some sixteen hundred years, made Romney Marsh what we now see it. It was they who first built upon the shingle where Dymchurch Wall now keeps the sea at bay, and their work was the "Rhee Wall"—the *rivi vallum* of their language—that, running from Appledore to Romney, kept the fresh water out of the land it was now their earnest endeavour to reclaim. Portus Lemanis, of course, was ruined, but, equally of course, not at once. How rarely does one actually picture the real length of the Roman stay in Britain, which actually comprised over four hundred years; or, to put it in a picturesque comparison, a period of time equal to that between our own day and the reign of Henry VIII. For half of their colonial period—say from a time corresponding to that between the reign of Queen Anne and that of Edward VII.—they were engaged in enclosing and draining the marsh, and there must have been ample time for the inhabitants of Portus Lemanis to realise the position. Did the Roman scheme, we wonder, allow them compensation?

By the time that their empire fell to pieces, and their troops and colonists were withdrawn from Britain, they had succeeded by degrees in altering this scene into a bog, and then into fenced-off enclosures intersected with drains and having a great reedy expanse of lake in the centre, where the wild fowl nested in myriads. Something very like this scene, although on a smaller scale, may now be observed at Slapton Sands, between Dartmouth and Torcross in South Devon, where a shingle bank divides the scene from a long length of a freshwater lake, choked with aquatic plants and teeming with wildlife.

This scene of reclamation must have reverted to a very wild condition in the savage centuries after the Romans had left, and we hear nothing of any further works until the eighth century, when the monks of Christ Church, Canterbury, were granted the western portion of the marsh, and reclaimed much of it around New Romney.

It was somewhere about this period, when it was difficult to convict a writer of untruth, that Nennius, Abbot of Bangor, in his *History of the Britons*, told his pleasant fable about Romney Marsh. His imagination was not limited by his ever having visited Kent, and so, sitting in the scriptorium at Bangor, he could give his lively fancy full play. He describes it as "the first marvel of Britain, for in it are sixty islands, with men living in them. It is girt by sixty rocks, and in every rock is an eagle's (not a mare's) nest. And sixty rivers flow into it, and yet there goes into the sea but one river, which is called the Limen." For a series of picturesque lies that would be difficult to beat, outside the *Arabian Nights*, whose tales do not pretend to be other than fiction.

It was by the efforts of the monastery of Christ Church that the harbour of New Romney, two miles farther down than the ancient Rother mouth, was begun, and, in spite of Danish incursions and frequent lapses into barbarism, the work went surely forward, so that in the Norman period, the eleventh and twelfth centuries, the marsh was grazing ground for sheep, settled and prosperous, with numerous villages and churches, whose Norman architecture bears witness to the truth of history, as written in dryasdust deeds and charters.

The Church derived a splendid profit from the enterprise with which it had thus developed its property. Fat fields yielded toll of rent and wool; the important harbour of New Romney collected rich shipping dues. And then!— then befell a series of the greatest tempests ever known on these shores—the storms of 1236, 1250, 1286, and 1334. The first two wrought much havoc, but the great February storm of 1286 was the worst, when the wind and the sea choked up the harbour with shingle and diverted the course of the Rother, and, tearing down the sea-defences, lay the hardly-won lands once more under salt water. This crowning disaster paralysed all effort. Only by degrees, and unaided, did the waters subside. The unfortunate inhabitants had lost all; many lost their lives; the port of Romney was crippled. Tradition even goes so far as to tell how fifty-two thousand persons were drowned in a tidal wave. Worst of all, the great monastery of Christ Church, ruled at that time by men more grasping than enterprising, expended nothing to make those misfortunes lighter. The port and harbour of New Romney, in especial, brought into flourishing existence by the statesmanlike policy of the early churchmen, was ruined by the later, who at this hour of need treated it merely as a source of revenue, and refused to undertake those works which, embarked upon in time, might have preserved its importance. Great shingle-banks filled the harbour entrance, and only the smallest vessels could enter. So affairs remained, the townsfolk feebly delving and clearing the obstructions, unaided, for close upon half a century, when the furious storm of 1334 undid all their work and finally crushed their spirit of resistance. At this time, also, the district was exposed to foreign attack.

Thus it was that, in the reign of Edward IV., the marsh was, for its better government and to induce settlement and reclamation of the drowned lands, placed under the control of the bailiff and jurats appointed by the charter of February 23rd, 1461. In the introduction to this measure, the marsh was declared to be "much deserted, owing to the danger resulting from foreign invasion and to the unwholesomeness of the soil and situation." To support that statement, and to show that this scheme was not altogether successful, comes the very interesting description by Lambarde, who, a hundred years later, says, "The place hath in it sundry villages, although not thick set, nor much inhabited, because it is *Hyeme malus, Aestate molestus, Nunquam bonus*—Evill in winter, grievous in summer, and never good"; or, in the once familiar Kentish phrase, the marsh provided "wealth without health," good grass but unwholesome air.

Freed from the paralysing ownership of the Church, on the Reformation an effort was made to encourage settlers in this almost deserted region by granting those who held land within its limits freedom from many of those imposts with incomprehensible names that must have made the lot of mediæval taxpayers unhappy. "Toll and tare," "scot and lot," "fifteen and subsidy," were the particular extortions excused to these adventurous persons, and to quote Lambarde again, "so many other charges as I suppose no one place within the Realm hath. All which was done (as it appeareth in the Charter itself) to allure men to inhabit the Marsh which they had before abandoned, partly for the unwholesomeness of the soil, and partly for fear of the enemie, which had often brent and spoyled them."

These inducements did not have much effect, for although many taxes were remitted, there was still that special local tax levied to provide funds for keeping the sea defences in repair, and that alone was, and still remains, a heavy burden on the land. Thus many of the deserted villages of the marsh were never re-populated, as we may still see in the ruined churches and waste sites in its midst.

But the marsh was not wholly devoid of population. As the waters subsided and grass grew again, so the flocks increased; and the ancient trade of smuggling, which began in the time of Edward I. in the illegal exportation of wool, flourished all the more from this being a lonely district in which it was difficult for strangers to find their way. This, the first phase in the long and varied history of smuggling, was then known as "owling," and the dangerous trade at once enlisted men fully as courageous and desperate as those who, in later ages, when lace, tea, tobacco, and brandy were the chief items in the contraband industry, terrorised the countryside and warred with the preventive service in many a midnight skirmish. "Owling" took its name from the signal-calls of the smugglers to one another on black and moonless nights. They imitated the weird shrieks of those nocturnal birds, and never was such a place for owls as Romney Marsh in the brave times of contraband.

The exportation of wool was at first only taxed, but later was entirely prohibited. The object aimed at in depriving the Continent of wool was the extinction of the foreign weaving industries, and the establishment of the clothing trade in this country. To insure the fleeces not being shipped abroad by men eager for personal gain and indifferent to patriotism or national policy, the taxes on bales varied from twenty to forty shillings in the reign of Edward I., but exportation was wholly forbidden by Edward III., whose Queen ardently desired to introduce colonies of Flemish weavers to use our home-grown wool within these shores. Punishments ranging from death down to mutilation of ears or hands were provided for those who infringed this severe law, but these penalties had few terrors for the marshfolk, secure in their boggy fastnesses. The marsh produced some wool, and the inland districts a great deal more, and every shearing season, impudently flaunting all laws and prohibitions, long lines of pack-horses, laden with woolpacks, found their way to New Romney and quiet places along this coast, on their way to France. For every new restrictive amendment of the laws the smuggling exporters of wool had an ingenious evasion, and so the contest went on for centuries. The law was the more successfully outwitted and defied because the landowners and every rural class were financially interested in the illegal trade. Although, as a special effort against wool leaving the country, shearers were at last required to shear only at certain specified times, and to register the number of fleeces, this provision was openly broken. In 1698 it was enacted that no man living within fifteen miles of the sea in Kent or Sussex should buy any wool, unless he entered into sureties that none of what he bought should be sold to any person within fifteen miles of the coast; and wool-growers were required to account for the number of fleeces they owned, and state the places where they were stored. But legislators might have saved themselves the trouble, for it was calculated that forty thousand packs of wool continued to be illegally conveyed annually to Calais. The Devil might as reasonably be expected to reprove sin as the local magistrates and persons in authority to suppress the lucrative trade in which they waxed rich.

Under such circumstances, the officials who were entrusted with the administration of these laws led a very hard life. They were the Ishmaels against whom every man's hand was raised, and the more strictly they performed their duty, by so much more were they hated. One striking incident has survived out of many such that must have happened. The mounted excise officers who in 1694 patrolled the district made a capture of ten men escorting a large pack-horse train of wool-bales to some pushing-off place for France, and haled them before his worship the Mayor of New Romney. Sworn information and due process of law were followed, and Mr. Mayor was desired to commit the captives to prison. Instead of doing so, he strained his discretionary powers to the utmost, and admitted them to bail. Possibly he had an interest in that very consignment thus put under embargo, or at the very least of it claimed friendship with, or was under neighbourly or business obligations to those to whom it did belong—so thoroughly bound up with smuggling was every detail of trade and intercourse in the marsh. This admission of the whole gang to bail was but the second act of the comedy, of which the seizure was the first, and it was followed by another, and a more stirring one. During the night the furious populace of Romney burst in upon the Revenue men, and so threatened them with violence that the Mayor's son advised them, in God's name, begone, lest worse befell.

Most excellent advice, and they take it. Half-dressed, and flinging themselves upon their horses in haste, they ride out of Romney with the whole town after them, and the town's pots and kettles hurtling in the air after pursued and pursuers alike. Jacob Rawlings, as good a freetrader as anyone, and hating an Exciseman as he ought to hate the Devil, is downed by a saucepan intended for a King's officer; Nehemiah Crutwell, who thinks good wool ought never to be taxed, has got a cut in the cheek from a brass skillet, flung with uncertain aim; the sconce of another is cracked by a broomstick intended for the crupper of one of the horses. Off they go into the night, pursued by fifty armed men, vowing death and destruction, and not until they have floundered across Guildford Level, and are come to Camber Point and Sussex, do their enemies draw off.

CHAPTER VII

ROMNEY MARSH (*continued*)

There is no fault to be found with the present condition of the road that leads from Warehorne to Snargate. It winds amazingly, but the surface is good and the width sufficient to keep the most inexpert drivers of traps or riders of cycles from steering into the black dykes that line it. Far otherwise, however, is it with the tracks that branch off boldly here and there and lure the unwary into extraordinary remotenesses where the guide-book measurements and acreage of the marsh seem a mockery, and its limits recede with every step. Lonely cottages, where the "lookers," or shepherds, or the dykers live, are passed at infrequent intervals, each one a forbidding box of dull brick, with its generally unkempt garden and numerous chickens, and its great pile of faggots or brushwood for winter's firing. In this wilderness may be found many of those deserted sites already mentioned; the shapeless walls of ruined churches alone telling silently of the great flood and the drowned villages. Eastbridge Chapel, Orgarswick, Blackmanstone, and Hope Chapel are the chief of these. Newchurch and Ivychurch are striking exceptions to this old tale of destruction. They belong to the same Early English period, with later additions, and are large, handsome structures. Standing on ground rising ever so slightly higher than the sites of their unfortunate neighbours, they escaped destruction, to tell us how well, and on how grand a scale they builded who first brought the marsh under cultivation.

Romney Marsh is still so greatly in a state of nature that the black-headed gull breeds freely in its reedy dykes, although, to be sure, the demand for plovers' eggs causes much havoc to be wrought among its nests by denizens of the neighbourhood, who earn a very excellent livelihood by supplying London poulterers. The simple native and the honest poulterer both do very well, and so long as the London consumer of expensive "plover's" eggs knows no better, why, no harm is done.

Snargate stands on that fine, straight, broad, and level road from Appledore to New Romney which bears the strongest evidence of having once been a raised causeway across the morasses, and is in fact identical with the Rhee Wall, already mentioned as having been built by the Romans to keep out the river Rother. "Snargate" was originally the name given to a sluice from the marsh into the river at this point. An inn, the church, a few old cottages, the vicarage—that is now the sum-total of Snargate, whose flint and stone battlemented church-tower peeps over the surrounding trees, and forms a pretty picture for a great distance down the long perspective of the road. A near approach shows it to be not only surrounded with trees, but hemmed in by them, and so closely that they obscure the light from the plain, leaded casement windows, and cast a green, mildewy, fungoid shade over all. Great gloomy churchyard yews, planted, perhaps, by the first church-builders, grow at close quarters and carpet the ground with thick and vivid moss, and two giant trees that look like pollard beeches, but on closer inspection are seen to be ashes, stand sentinel by the south porch, and lift eerie phalanginous branches dramatically upright.

It is a fine old church, built in the graceful Early English style, and on quite a large scale; but now uncared for and horribly damp. When, having obtained the keys, you swing back the groaning door, the reek of the dampness smites you coldly in the face, and the odour of it produces a sneeze that goes hollowly reverberating up and down the mildewed interior. Emptiness and damp are the interior characteristics of Snargate church—its pavements slimy with moisture, the walls alternately livid and green with it. It is not surprising that Barham preferred to live at Warehorne.

SNARGATE.

Brenzett village is larger and livelier than Snargate. From it Brookland, Ivychurch, and Newchurch are most easily reached—the first, on the right-hand side of this causeway road to New Romney, in Walling Marsh; the others to the left, in the Marsh of Romney. Brookland is distant one mile from the main road, on a by-way that, if you follow it long enough, brings you dustily into Rye; dustily, because the traffic that resorts to Brookland station cuts up the surface to an astonishing extent; astonishing, because that traffic is necessarily of small dimensions, seeing that this is merely a branch railway leading to the very verge and outer rim of the world at Dungeness. An infallible sign of this scarcity of road traffic is the action of the keeper of the level crossing by the station, whom one suspects to be also station-master, ticket-collector, porter, and signalman combined. He touches his hat to the passing tourist, and, glad to hear the voice of a stranger, exchanges remarks on the weather.

BROOKLAND.

From afar off, along the flat road, the whimsical bell-tower of Brookland church rises, like some strange portent. If the stranger has not heard of it before, he speculates, perplexed, as to what it can possibly be, for, seen in silhouette against the sky, it presents the weirdest kind of outline. Imagine three old-fashioned candle-extinguishers, placed one upon the other, and you have that odd campanile very closely imitated. It stands apart from the church, is of massive oak framing, weatherboarded, and thickly and most liberally tarred. The wildest local legends exist, purporting to account for this freak, the most specious of all telling how the builder of the church finding he had lost by the contract, set this up in place of the stone tower originally contemplated. The real reason for this detached wooden belfry is found in the old-time nature of the site, too waterlogged to be capable of giving support to so heavy a structure as a stone tower. A wicked old satirical allusion to this unusual feature, still current in the village—or perhaps rather, considering its nature, in the surrounding villages—declares that when a bachelor and a maid are married in Brookland church, the belfry will leap up and occupy a place on the roof. As marriages here are not uncommon, and the belfry keeps its place, this, it will be allowed, is a grievous saying. An old writer, with a naive assumption of innocence, noting this example of local humour, pretends not to understand the libellous gibe. "What it doth portend," he remarks, "I know not." He should have inquired, say, at Brenzett—or, indeed, anywhere save at Brookland, whose inhabitants are still touchy on the subject; as well they may be, since every passing stranger, posted in local lore, lets off a joke or makes jocular inquiry.

Returning to the main road, a signpost directs into the heart of Romney Marsh, by way of Ivychurch and Newchurch. Ivychurch, whose tower is dimly visible from the road in the soft atmosphere of the marsh, is a mile and

69

a half distant, and stands as isolated from the world as a place well may be and yet remain a "going concern." What is there of Ivychurch? A few farmsteads, a few more cottages, an oast-house or so, a village inn, and an amazingly large church. Apart from New Romney church, which is that of a town and therefore not comparable with that of this rural parish, the great church of Ivychurch is by far the largest in the whole district, and fully deserves to be called the Marshland Cathedral. It could accommodate, fifty times over, the present population of the parish, and the irresistible inference is that this must, six hundred years ago, when the great church was built, have been the most densely peopled region of the marsh. Nowadays, like all its fellow churches, it is damp and mouldy and a world too large. Nay, more: its vast empty interior is falling into decay, and the north aisle is made to serve the purpose of a coal-cellar; while, because the windows are broken, the wildfowl of this "recondite region" have made it a favourite roosting-place. It is an eerie experience, having procured the keys and unlocked the door, to be met with a tremendous whirring of wings, and to be almost knocked down with the surprise of a moorhen flying in one's face. Funds are accumulating for a restoration of this church; but, unless the people come back to the land, why expend so much good money? Better were it that this should go the way of the other ruined churches of the marsh if there be none to worship. The wheel of fortune, however, still turns. God grant the time be at hand when the yellowing corn becomes again that predominant feature in the landscape it never has been in the eyes of the present generation; that the farmer may again find his industry pay, and we be no longer dependent upon the foreigner for our food supplies.

IVYCHURCH.

NEWCHURCH, ON ROMNEY MARSH: "THIS RECONDITE REGION; THIS FIFTH QUARTER OF THE GLOBE."

Newchurch, nearly three miles farther into the marsh, was new seven hundred years ago, when the church was built. It is second only in size to Ivychurch, with the same lichenous damp,

but better cared for, and the centre of a quite considerable village, as villages go in these parts. There must actually be sufficient inhabitants in the parish to quarter fill the building! Newchurch makes a pretty picture, thoroughly characteristic of the marsh. From it the eye ranges to the wooded cliffs at Bilsington, to Aldington Knoll, and to Lympne, with its castle and church, looking fairy-like and ethereal in the shimmering light of a summer afternoon; or in the other direction to where the marsh is bounded by the sea. The picture of Newchurch itself is seen here, and is more eloquent than mere words can be. In it you perceive how this is an epitome of the marsh, with windmill and rushy dyke in the foreground, and farmsteads, rickyards and church, companionable together, and in appearance mutually dependent, in middle distance: the infinite levels of this interesting district appearing in the background. It is not by mere chance or by any figment of literary imagination that farms and church here look so dependent upon one another. They actually were so in the marsh, much more than is indicated by that tithing of the unhappy farmer customary all over the country. It was the Church, in the form of the monastery of Christ Church, Canterbury, that originally reclaimed the marsh and brought it under cultivation, and the Church was, by consequence, landlord. Long years of patient labour had resulted in winning these lands for agriculture, and the monastery fully earned the profits it eventually secured from its long-continued enterprise. Its piety was of two kinds,—of that practical sort which makes two blades of grass grow where but one grew before, and thus improves our temporal condition in this vale of tears; and of that spiritual and intellectual variety which, having founded settlements for the husbandmen, saw to it that his immortal as well as his earthly part should have due sustenance. This is no place to tell how in the course of centuries that Church fell away from its high ideals: here still survive neighbourly farm and parish place of worship, to prove that they once existed.

It is here, in the middle of the marsh, that you perceive how little given to change are the local methods. Sheep are still to be found here in thousands, and still tended, as from time immemorial, by that variety of shepherd known in these parts as a "looker." Ingoldsby names the manservant of Thomas Marsh of Marston, "Ralph Looker," and derived the name, doubtless, from this local title for shepherd.

The terms of a "looker's" employment are curious, and look wretchedly poor, but as they have survived, and show no signs of being revised in these times when labour is scarce on the farms and farmers eagerly compete for help, they cannot be worse than methods of paying shepherds in other parts of the country. A "looker" does everything connected with sheep-tending at an inclusive payment of one shilling and sixpence an acre per annum. For this he looks after the flocks, sees them through the horrors of the lambing season, shears them in summer, succours them in winter, and cures their ailments throughout the year. The sum seems pitiful, but when calculated on farms of six hundred acres or so, works out fairly well.

One comes to love the marsh, to delight in its byways, and to welcome opportunities for extended exploration. From Newchurch it is easily possible to find a way back to the main road without retracing one's footsteps. That way lies near the spot marked on ordnance maps as "Blackmanstone Chapel," a ruin so thoroughly ruinated that it is difficult to find—and not worth seeing when found. Blackmanstone Chapel was apparently founded by one Blacheman, who held the manor in the time of Edward the Confessor, but, in common with many such chapels, it seems to have been founded more for the repose of a single erring soul than to satisfy any crying spiritual need of the neighbourhood. The adjoining parish of St. Mary the Virgin is more fortunate. It keeps its ancient church in excellent condition. On its pavement the curious may note an epitaph to one Daniel Langdon, "Common Expenditor" of Romney Marsh, 1750.

The cautious explorer of the marsh is careful to carry his nosebag with him, in the shape of some pocketable light refreshment, for the inns are infrequent, and the farm-folk, although hospitable enough, cannot always supply even the most modest demands of the stranger. Milk even—that unfailing product of a farm—is not always to be had, for the morning's supply may already have been sent off to the nearest railway station, and the five o'clock afternoon milking hour be not yet come. Moreover, farmers generally entering into a contract to supply a certain quantity cannot always afford to sell even a single glass. As for farmhouse bread and cheese, dismiss from your mind all thoughts of home-baked bread or local cheese in these times. The bread will often be a tin loaf from the baker's of Ashford, Hythe, or Littlestone; and the cheese—well, here is the apology of a farmer's wife: "I'm sorry we've no Dutch cheese, but here is some American; we think it very good." Can such things be? you ask. *Can* they be, indeed? Are they not the commonplace experiences of all those few who really explore the innermost recesses of the country and feel the pulse and count the heart-beats of rural life? Is there not something radically wrong with England when a farmer's wife can make such a speech as that, and not think it strange? In the dying words of the late Lord Winchilsea, a true friend of farming, "God save Agriculture!" when in an English dairying district the farmers buy Dutch and American cheese.

But that is not the only alien article in the farmhouses. Tawdry German glassware and "ornamental" china "decorate" the "best parlour," and the doleful wailings of American organs on Sundays give evidence of the religious instincts of the farmer's family and agonise the unhappy wayfarer. Old England is certainly being cosmopolitanised (good word!) in every direction; here is another instance, for what do we see on the barn-walls and posting-stations but the announcement, addressed to the rustics, of a "Fête Champêtre" to be held in aid of a church restoration fund. In the days before Hodge left off saying "beant" and took to using the more cultivated phrase "is not," like the Squire and the Parson, he would—supposing him able to read at all—have asked, wonderingly, "What be this 'ere Feet Shampeter?"—and that would have been a very learned Squire or Parson who could have correctly explained the meaning.

CHAPTER VIII

OLD AND NEW ROMNEY AND DYMCHURCH

Returning from this excursion into the intimate things of the marsh, and making for New Romney, attention is arrested by the view of a group of a church and two houses at a little distance from the road. This the map proclaims to be Old Romney, that sometime seaport, busy and prosperous in Saxon times, before ever the Normans came to follow the retreating sea and to found New Romney, a mile and more away. Old Romney is so very old that it has forgotten its past, and antiquaries can tell little or nothing of it; but with our vision illumined by legitimate imagination, we can picture that old port in no uncertain way, perched upon its slight eminence and overlooking the mingling of salt water and fresh at this long-vanished mouth of the Rother; the Saxon ships beached on the shingle-falls, or stuck fast in the alluvial mud of still bayous. Where those keels came to anchor, the ploughman drives his furrow, and where the wooden houses of that old town stood, the broad fields of oats, beans, and turnips ripen in the sun. The population of the whole parish of Old Romney, with its outlying hamlets and cottages, numbers not more than a hundred and fifty, and of village there is but this lonely group of church, vicarage, and two farmhouses. The church itself, Norman and Early English though it be, is of the rural type, and thus tells us that already, when it was built, the place had sunk into insignificance. There it stands, on its scarcely perceptible knoll, its broad-based tower, constructed of flint and shingle grouting, eloquent of the Has Been, and still indifferent, as for seven hundred years past, to the To Be. Dynasties, social conditions, the whole polity of a nation, have changed, time and again, since that old tower first arose beside this Rhee Wall road. All the little injustices, oppressions, and disasters, all the joys and sorrows of seven centuries, all those flouts of cynic Circumstance that in their time seem so great and poignant, have passed it by, and still, with its immemorial attendant yew-tree, it looks upon this ancient road, calmly contemptuous of the wayfarers that come and go. There is that in this merely rural church which impresses one much more deeply than—or in an altogether different way from—the sight of a cathedral. The great minster means intellectual and religious exaltation; here a sense of the futility of men and things—of the evanescent nature of those who build and of the astounding permanency and indifference of the things they rear—clutches the heart with the grip of ice. Not here the *sursum corda* of the pilgrim, but the gloom of the pessimist and the tears of those who sorrow for the littleness of our little span are called forth by the solitude, the isolation and minatory prominence of this marshland church. For though it be neighboured by

74

farmsteads, the brooding spirit of the place is communicated to them, rather than their domestic cheerfulness irradiating its aloofness. In fine, only the stolid and the unimaginative should live at Old Romney, whose minor key deepens into a sadder intensity when day draws to its close, as the shadows lengthen and the cattle come, lowing, home to byre.

OLD ROMNEY.

I would do much to avoid Old Romney at such time o' day, coming to it by preference in early morning, when the summer sun is hot upon the earth, but not so hot nor so long risen that it has had time to dry the dew upon the fragrant wild thyme of the grass. Then there is hope in the atmosphere, and the Past does not lie with so dead a weight upon the Present and the Future.

But to continue to New Romney. There, on the way, across the level, seen dimly through the heat-haze, and scarce distinguishable from a ragged clump of trees, rises the shattered wall that is the sole relic of Hope Chapel, one of the ruined endeavours of the marsh. Hope All Saints is traditionally said to have been the first settlement in the district, and named "Hope"—it is a simple, artless belief—as expressive at once of the anxieties and the trustfulness of those original settlers, who selected that comprehensive dedication of "All Saints" with the businesslike idea of enjoying as extended a patronage as possible among the bright and shining ones of the New Jerusalem. Alas! for the protection thus sought. Hope has been deserted time out of mind, and the walls of its chapel are a shapeless and solitary mass. Such also is the condition of Mydley Chapel, in Dunge Marsh, on the right-hand side of the road, whose ruined gable-end is seen standing out prominently, like an inverted Y.

Within sight, surrounded by that almost invariable circlet of trees which seems to lovingly enfold the churches, the villages, and the townlets of the marsh, and to shelter them from the cold blasts of change, as also from those of the weather, is New Romney, the four angle-tourelles or dwarf pinnacles of its church tower—not one quite the counterpart of any of its fellows—

75

prominent above all else.

Rounding an acute bend in the road, and passing a few scattered nondescript sheds and outbuildings, we come with surprising suddenness into the old Cinque Port that is so surprisingly called "new." A dog dozing in the middle of the broad, empty street, a piano being somewhere injuriously practised upon, the sound of a laugh in the parlour of an old inn—these sights and sounds comprise the life and movement of New Romney on a mid-day of this midsummer in the early twentieth century.

The newness of New Romney is now only a battered and outworn figure of speech, to be taken relatively and with reference to that Old Romney we have just left. What the streets of New Romney were like when it really was new— about the time of the Norman Conquest—we cannot conceive; how they looked when it had already grown to a respectable age, when the Late Norman church of St. Nicholas was built, we can form no idea. But it is certain that this was once a town of goodly size and great prosperity. At the time when the Cinque Ports were constituted, Romney was thought worthy to be of the company, and to be equal fellow with Hastings, Sandwich, Dover, and Hythe; but so early as 1351 it was so decayed by reason of its misfortunes at the hands of tempests and the contrary sea-currents that shoaled and silted-up its harbour, that the unfortunate port could not send out its quota of ships for the national defence, and was penalised accordingly, losing for a time many of its Cinque Port privileges. When Queen Elizabeth visited the town, and granted it the empty honour of a Mayor and Corporation, it was very much in the condition it occupies now. Of its five churches, only one—the one still standing—was left, the sea was two miles distant, and her "poor town of Romney" would have been sore put to it to do her honour, except for the liberality of certain substantial men whose purses were equal to the heavy calls such Royal visits made. But, it may be asked, if the town were in such sore case, whence came the wealth of those substantial burgesses? Ay, whence? Why, from that unchartered industry of smuggling of whose history we have already heard so much. The port and town might decay, but for centuries before Elizabeth's time and until the first half of the nineteenth century had almost gone, the "owling" trade in the exportation of wool, and the import smuggling of exciseable articles, enriched many a highly-respectable family and kept a whole army of longshore loafers in comfortable circumstances. Strangers with astonishment saw substantial mansions in these wilds, eloquent in their every appointment of a high degree of prosperity, and Ireland, writing on Kent at the beginning of the nineteenth century, could not comprehend the existence here, where there was no distinguishable commerce, of the "numbers of stout, hale-looking men" who were always loafing about, without any visible occupation. If Mr. Ireland had walked abroad o' nights, he would have discovered that those aimless persons were then very busily employed, and he would probably have received a crack over the head from one or other of them, if thought too curious. The smuggling fraternity did not welcome curious strangers.

But Ireland can scarce have been so ignorant as not to comprehend so very obvious a thing. Either he was not sufficiently frank in his writings, or else assumed a clumsy and not easily-detected archness. For the thing was notorious and patent to everyone. Long before and after his day, Hasted, the historian of Kent, described New Romney as a town of one hundred and eighty houses and one thousand inhabitants, "chiefly such as follow a contraband trade between this kingdom and France." But gone are those times, and the town is now too listless either to grow, or to die and so make an end.

The country is in the middle of the town at Romney. The stranger who glances down the quiet street can see the cows grazing round the corner; "baa" comes from flocks and herds, in successful competition with the rare ting-a-ling of alarum-bells on shop-doors, infrequently opened; and the crows and jackdaws hold a noisy witenagemot among the embowering trees of the churchyard—the "God's Acre" of this one remaining church of St. Nicholas, that patron saint who impartially looked after the interests of sailors and thieves. Thieves were, indeed, in the Middle Ages known by the polite title of "St. Nicholas' clerks"—hence perhaps the vulgar term of "nicking" for stealing.

NEW ROMNEY.

It is a fine old Norman building, this church of St. Nicholas, with a tower arcaded and panelled in the well-known Norman style, and a grand, black-browed, ponderous interior, infinitely eloquent of old-time importance. The old altar tomb to Richard Stuppeneye, Jurat of the Marsh in 1509, in times before Mayors of Romney, stands at the east end of the south aisle, and was the spot where the business of the town was transacted in days before a town hall was erected; times when men thought it no ill to employ the house of God in between whiles for certain secular purposes. Stuppeneye's tomb, as an inscription states, was erected by his great-grandson in 1622, "for the use of the ancient meeting and election of Maior and Jurats of this port towne." And surely, if there be anything in associations and surroundings the town's business was like to be hallowed by the place where it was conducted, just as the annual election of a mayor beside the worthy Stuppeneye's resting-place should have secured a fitting magistrate. Let no one cite the mayor who sympathised with and aided the "owlers" as an instance of an unfit representative being chosen, for no one outside the Revenue ever thought any form of smuggling sinful. But old customs were broken some nine years since, and no longer is the mayor chosen beside the tomb of that worthy jurat.

Close beside this monument may be noticed, on the floor, a stone to "Edward Elsted, many years Riding Officer of this Place," who died in 1757, aged 51, doubtless, if he was a true and faithful servant of the Revenue, to the great joy of the smuggling interests of the town; for by the term "Riding Officer," we are to understand a mounted official of the Preventive Service to be indicated.

For the rest, New Romney may easily be dismissed. There is the "New Inn," with a frontage perhaps not older than one century, but with an interior that was only new five hundred years ago, where the smuggling cult used to hold convivial and profit-sharing meetings; there is the Town Hall next door, and there is the broad street with never a new building in it, or anywhere at all in the town. Sandwich is commonly held up as an example of a Cinque Port utterly decayed and dead as Queen Anne, or as the Pharaohs, or anything or anyone of whose demise there cannot possibly be any doubt, but there are new houses and other unmistakable signs of a living existence there, while here the town, reduced to the merest existence, simply continues mechanically, like a clock not yet run down. It is not an unpleasing—nay, it is even an interesting—place, but it gives an odd, weather-beaten, bleak impression, not perhaps so much to the eye as to the mind. It is possible to visit New Romney when the thermometer registers eighty in the shade, and for the mind to convey that bleak impression so acutely to the senses that the body shivers.

If, however, you want something really gaunt and shivery, why then, Littlestone-on-Sea will give all you desire in that sort, in full measure and brimming over. Littlestone-on-Sea might with equal propriety and more exact descriptiveness be named Littlestone-at-the-World's-End. It stands on the shingle-banks that have been thrown up by the sea to ruin Romney, and it is a mere line of sad grey stucco houses with their faces to the immensity of the sea, their backs to the emptiness of the marsh, and their skylights looking up into the vastness of the sky. The place is a resort of golfers in summer, an emptiness in winter, and all the year round an eyesore to those who fare the road between Romney and Dymchurch, and cannot fail to observe those gaunt houses in the distance, notching the coast-line in a hateful commonplace of detached-and semi-detachedness.

Here, along this coastwise road, between this point and Hythe, we make close acquaintance with the Martello towers. A ready way of describing the shape of one of these towers is to picture it as an inverted flower-pot. The proportions of height and circumference are very nearly the same, and what architects and builders would call the "batter"—*i.e.*, the narrowing slope of the sides—runs at very closely the same angle.

A MARTELLO TOWER.

They are just upon a century old. Built solidly, of honest brickwork through and through, in the days of the Great Terror, no enemy's fire has ever been directed against them, but several have been used as targets for the heavy ordnance and high explosives of the modern gunners of Lydd and Dungeness, and, with a great deal of labour and at huge expense, at last destroyed. Some few, also, have been undermined and ruined by the encroachments of the sea. There were originally seventy-six of these towers, costing from £10,000 to £20,000 apiece, according to size. The usual size is thirty feet in height, with a diameter of forty feet at the base, diminishing to thirty at the top. They are in two storeys, with a bomb-proof roof formerly surmounted by a cannon mounted on a swivel-carriage. The walls vary from a thickness of nine feet on the seaward side to six on the landward, which would not be so greatly exposed to assault. Their name is said to derive from that circular fort at Martella, in Corsica, captured only after a long and desperate resistance in the time of Nelson. It has been left for modern times to thoroughly vindicate the plan of the military engineers who designed this first line of defence along an unprotected coast. Fortunately, there has never been any occasion to put these to the test, and it was not until the same blockhouse principle was introduced on the veldt in the second Boer War, that the weary campaign was brought at last to a close.

This tower, standing at the entrance to Dymchurch, behind the famous Wall, has been put to a whimsical use, for it is in occupation by a poor family, whose rent of half-a-crown a week, due to the War Office, is guaranteed by the vicar. A Martello tower makes a squalid home. Very little light can struggle through the deep and narrow embrasures, and the interior is grimly suggestive of a mausoleum. The ragged duds drying from flaunting clothes-lines, the position of the tower planted in a scrubby waste, with domestic refuse strewed about, and the stark nakedness of the brick, combine to make an inglorious and repellent picture.

DYMCHURCH WALL.

Here begins that famous three miles length of bulwark against the sea, Dymchurch Wall. Witches no longer skim across it on their broomsticks, but when the wind comes booming out of the Channel from a lowering sky, and the seagulls fly screaming low upon the water, you will, quite possibly, not believe and tremble, but will understand—what you will by no means comprehend only by reading the printed page—that it is, to the imaginative, a "whisht" place. The modern marshmen are not imaginative, fancy does not breed in their brains, and all they see in a storm is the chance of a rich aftermath of driftwood; but their forebears heard a voice in every wind, and handled every besom with that respect due to a thing which, under cover of night, might have been, and might be again, an unholy sort of Pegasus, bound for some Satanic aerial *levée*.

Dymchurch village shelters very humbly behind this Wall, from whose summit one looks down upon it, or, on the other side, down upon a long, vanishing perspective of solitary sands and blackened, rotting timber groynes. The Wall is about twelve feet high, with a curved, concave "apron" of boulders toward the sea, and an abrupt turfy slope on the inland face. The summit affords a fine continuous walk, and has been an undisguised earthen and grassy path since a few years ago, when £35,000 worth of paving-stones, provided to make it look neat and town-like, were swept away to sea in a storm.

DYMCHURCH WALL.

Bungalows have now begun to appear here and there inside the Wall adjoining Dymchurch, for there are summer visitors to whom the solitude and the unconstrained freedom of the empty sands are welcome; but, situated as they are, close against the inner face of the Wall, they have the blankest sort of outlook.

CHAPTER IX

HYTHE AND FOLKSTONE

From Dymchurch, five miles of excellent road bring one into Hythe, that old Cinque Port whose early Saxon name means "harbour," and thus tells those among us who are thinking men how important a place it was of old. "*The* Harbour," definitely and emphatically it was, of capital importance in those far-away times when Sandwich, Romney, Dover, Folkestone, and others were of less moment; but even by the time the Cinque Ports came into existence it had declined to inferior rank among its brethren, and when Dover was required to furnish twenty-one ships for the defence of the nation, and Winchelsea and Hastings respectively ten and six, Hythe, Sandwich, Rye,and Romney were assessed at only five each. Where is that harbour of which some vestiges remained to the time of Elizabeth? that haven which, according to Leland, was "strayt for passage owt of Boloyn?" Where but choked up, embedded, and deeply overlaid beneath a mile-long waste of shingle! The glory of that storied port is buried "full fathom five." Everywhere is shingle. A world of it expands before the vision as one comes out of the marsh towards the town, and Martello towers and forlorn congeries of more modern forts stand islanded in midst of it. From the sunlit glare of this waste the road enters Hythe, through an exquisitely beautiful woodland, open and unfenced from the highway, with the landward ridge of hills and the Military Canal approaching on the left.

"Hythe hath bene," says Leland, "a very greate towne yn length, ande conteyned IIII paroches, that now be clene destroied." The greatest surviving evidence of that ancient estate is the one remaining church of St. Leonard, which tops the hill behind the High Street and is the crown and distinguishing mark of Hythe from afar off. It is chiefly of Early English architecture, and an exquisite example of its period, with a noble chancel like the choir of a cathedral, and a remarkable crypt or undercroft, stacked with a neatly-disposed heap of many hundreds of skulls and large quantities of human bones. No one knows in any definite manner how, why, or when these gruesome relics were brought here, but legendary lore tells how they are the remains of those who were slain in some uncertain fight—so uncertain that whether between Britons and Romans, Romano-British and Saxons, or Saxons and Danes is not stated. Borrow, in his *Lavengro*, plumps for Danes, more perhaps because he had a prejudice for that hypothesis than from any evidence he could have produced, if asked. That many of the owners of those skulls did actually meet a violent death is quite evident in the terrific gashes they exhibit. One may see these poor relics for threepence, and Hythe does a roaring trade with the morbid in photographs of the shocking collection; but it were better they were decently buried and given rest from the handling and the flippant comments of the shallow-minded crowd.

One refuses further to discuss skulls in the holiday sunshine of Hythe, whose long, narrow street is cheerful and pulsing with life. Hythe street is one of those humanly interesting old thoroughfares which one is inclined, in the mass, to call picturesque; but on reflection it is seen to be really always about to become so, as you advance, and never to actually arrive at any very remarkably picturesque climax. The Georgian town hall, standing on pillars, is interesting, and so, too, is that queer little building called the "Smugglers' Nest," claiming to be a look-out place of some of the many "free-traders" who carried on operations from the town. For the rest, Hythe is old-fashioned and by no means overwhelmed, as many of its neighbours are, by modernity. Here the four separate and distinct streams of seafaring, military, agricultural, and shop-keeping life pool their interests and mingle amicably enough, under the interested observation of a fifth contingent, the summer visitors who find the unconventional attractions of the shingle and the unspoiled place more to their taste than the modish charms of Folkestone.

THE "SMUGGLERS' NEST," HYTHE.

Just where Hythe ends and Seabrook begins, the Military Canal comes to a dusty and somewhat stagnant conclusion on the flat foreshore. Lest the dreaded invader should not play the game properly, and meanly attempt to land his troops on the open and undefended beach beyond the tract of country cut off by that "not very practicable ditch," a Martello tower was set up on the little shoulder of a hill overlooking this spot, and there it remains to this day. A grey, grim, giant hotel stands isolated out upon the shingle-banks, and would offer a splendid mark for any modern invader who should descend upon the coast and do the neighbourhood the kindness to blow its hideous presence away.

HYTHE, FROM THE ROAD TO SANDGATE.

That stranger who might pass from Hythe to Sandgate and know nothing of the separate existence of Seabrook would have every excuse, for it bears every outward appearance of belonging to one or other. It is largely a recent development, and in so far a pleasing one, for its pretty new gabled seaside red-brick cottages, giving immediately upon the shore, are in the best of taste and have delightful gardens, where the little bare-legged boys and girls of the visitors sit in the sun or sprawl, book-reading, upon the steps. Opposite these, evidences of an enlightened taste, some grey "compo" villas cast a gloom over those who glance upon them and tell us how stupid were those times of some thirty years ago, when such sad-faced houses arose everywhere at the seaside in this grey climate that calls aloud for the cheerfulness of colour in building.

Sandgate, into which Seabrook insensibly merges, sits so close upon the shore that it is credibly reported the lodging-house landladies live on the upper floors of their houses in those empty winter months when the winds blow great guns and the seas come pouring into the basements, bringing with them large deposits of that plentiful shingle, fragments of sea-wall, and twisted remnants of promenade railings. Year in and year out, the sea and the Local Board, or Urban District Council, or whatever may be the name of the authority that rules Sandgate, play a never-ending game. In the summer the authority builds up a sea-wall, and, in effect, says to the sea, "You can't smash *that*!" And the sea sparkles and drowses in the sun and laps lazily upon the shore, and artfully agrees. But when the visitors have all gone home, and the equinoctial gales go ravening up and down the Channel, then Londoners open their morning papers and say to their wives, "You remember that sea-wall at

Sandgate, my dear, where we used to sit in the shade: it was entirely washed away yesterday by the sea!" But by the time their next holiday comes round there is a newer wall there, on an improved pattern. That, too, is either utterly destroyed in the following winter and flung in fragments into neighbouring gardens, or else, with the roadway and the kerbs and lamp-posts, the pillar-boxes and the whole bag of tricks, swept out to sea and lost.

And so the game goes on. It is a costly one, and a heartbreaking for those folks who have semi-basement breakfast-rooms and ever and again experience the necessity of excavating their furniture out of the shingle-filled rooms, like so many Layards digging out the Assyrian relics of Nimroud and Baalbec. When such things can be, the desire of adjoining Folkestone for Sandgate and the determination of Sandgate not to be included within the municipal boundaries of its great neighbour are not readily to be understood.

Dramatic things happen at Sandgate. Vessels are cast away upon the road, their bowsprits coming in at the front doors, while shipwrecked mariners, instead of being flung upon an iron-bound coast, are projected against the palisades of the front gardens. At such times the variety of jettisoned cargo that comes ashore is remarkable. One day it will be a consignment of Barcelona nuts; another, a ship-load of boots; what not, indeed, from the jostling commerce that goes up and down that crowded sea-highway, the Channel. When the *Benvenue* was wrecked inshore here, at the close of 1891, and lay a menace to passing ships, that happened which sent Sandgate sliding and cracking in all directions. The wreck was blown up with dynamite, and soon afterwards the clayey clifflet that forms the foundation for the north side of Sandgate's one street slipped suddenly down, wrecking some houses and cracking many others from roof to foundation. Many, including the London newspapers, thought it was an earthquake.

Since then, Sandgate has largely altered, and instead of being rather an abject attempt at a seaside resort, has been brightened by re-building and cheered by the overflow to it from Folkestone's overbrimming cup of prosperity. Still stands Sandgate Castle on the sea-shore, one of Henry VIII.'s obese, tun-bellied blockhouses, very much in shape like that portly Henry himself, as we may safely declare now that Tudors no longer rule the land; but the very thought would have been treason, and its expression fatal, in that burly monarch's own day.

There is a choice of ways into Folkestone—by steeply-rising Sandgate Hill, or by the flat lower road, where a modern toll-gate stands to exact its dues for the convenience. This way the cyclist saves the climb, and pilgrims in general are spared the villa roads of the hill approach to the town, coming to it instead through pleasant woods, with the tangled abandon of the Leas undercliff rising up to the left.

Folkestone chiefly interests the Ingoldsby pilgrim because of that eloquent and humorous description of the old town to be found in "The Leech of Folkestone." There was then no new and fashionable town to be described, and the place was "a collection of houses which its maligners call a fishing-town, and its well-wishers a watering-place. A limb of one of the Cinque Ports, it has (or lately had) a corporation of its own, and has been thought considerable enough to give a second title to a noble family. Rome stood on seven hills—Folkestone seems to have been built upon seventy. Its streets, lanes, and alleys—fanciful distinctions without much real difference—are agreeable enough to persons who do not mind running up and down stairs; and the only inconvenience at all felt by such of its inhabitants as are not asthmatic is when some heedless urchin tumbles down a chimney or an impertinent pedestrian peeps into a garret window.

"At the eastern extremity of the town, on the sea-beach, and scarcely above high-water mark, stood, in the good old times, a row of houses, then denominated 'Frog Hole.' Modern refinement subsequently euphemised the name into 'East-street'; but 'what's in a name?'—the encroachments of Ocean have long since levelled all in one common ruin."

FOLKESTONE.

Nothing of the sort has happened. East Street is still there, and "East Street" yet, but no one has ventured to identify any house with that occupied by that compounder of medicines, "of somewhat doubtful reputation, but comparative opulence," Master Erasmus Buckthorne, "the effluvia of whose drugs from within, mingling agreeably with the 'ancient and fishlike smells' from without, wafted a delicious perfume throughout the neighbourhood."

It was to this picturesquely-described place that the Master Thomas Marsh of the legend and his man Ralph wended their way to consult that learned disciple of Esculapius with the fly-blown reputation; coming to it by "paths then, as now, most pseudonymously dignified with the name of roads."

Folkestone, the fisher-village, the "Lapis Populi" of the Romans and the "Fulchestane" of Domesday Book—stood in a pleasant country now quite lost sight of, built over, and bedevilled by the interminable brick and mortar of the great and fashionable seaside resort that Folkestone is at this day. It lay, that fisher-haven, in a hollow at the seaward end of a long valley bordered by the striking hills of the chalk downs that are only now to be glimpsed by journeying a mile or so away from the sea-shore, past the uttermost streets, but were then visible at every point. Down this valley came, trickling and prattling in summer, or raging in winter, a little stream that, as it approached the sea, flowed in between the crazy tenements of the fisher-folk and smugglers who then formed the sole population—who then were the only folk —of Folkestone. This was the "Pent Stream," which found its way into the

88

sea obscurely enough, oozing insignificantly through the pebbles where the Stade and the Fishmarket now stand, by the harbour. Alas! for that forgotten rill; it is now made to mingle its waters with a sewer, and to flow under Tontine Street in a contaminated flood.

It is true that the small natural harbour was improved so early as 1810, or thereabouts, by Telford, but it was not until after 1844, when the South-Eastern Railway was opened, that Folkestone began to grow, and the original village began to be enclosed within the girdle of a "resort" quite alien from it in style, thought, and population.

There is no love felt for modern Folkestone by the inhabitants of the old town, who resent the prices to which things have been forced up by the neighbourhood of the over-wealthy, and resent still more the occasional descent from the fashionable Leas of dainty parties bent on exploring the queer nooks, and amusing themselves with a sight of the quaint characters, that still abound by the fishing-harbour. To those parties, every waterside lounger who sports a peaked cap and a blue jersey, and, resting his arms upon the railings by the quay and gazing inscrutably out to the horizon, presents a broad stern to the street, is a fisherman, and the feelings of a pilot, taken for a mere hauler upon nets and capturer of soles and mackerel, are often thus outraged.

THE STADE, FOLKESTONE.

For the spiritual benefit of the fisher-folk and others of the old town, there is planted, by the Stade, a "St. Peter's Mission," established there by well-meaning but stupid folk who look down, actually and figuratively, from the modern town upon this spot, and appear to think it a sink of iniquity. But iniquities are not always, or solely, resident in sinks; they have been found, shameless and flourishing, in high places. There are those among the fisher population who take the creature comforts—the coals and the blankets—of the mission, and pocket the implied affront; but there are also those others who, with clearer vision or greater independence of character, do not scruple to think and say that a mission for the salvation of many in that new town that so proudly crowns the cliffs would be more appropriate. "What," asked an indignant fisherman—"what makes them 'ere hotels pay like they does?" and he answered his own query in language that shall not be printed here. "If them as goes there all had to show their marriage-lines first," he concluded, "it's little business they'd do"; and his remarks recalled and illuminated the story of a week-end frequenter of one of the great caravanserais whose Saturday to Monday spouses were so frequently changed that even the seared conscience of a German hotel-manager was revolted.

Folkestone's fishing-harbour is wonderfully picturesque. Beside it stands the Stade, a collection of the quaintest, craziest old sail-lofts and warehouses, timbered and tarred and leaning at all sorts of angles. Down in the harbour itself the smacks cluster thickly. The rise and fall of the tide here is so much as eighteen feet, and at the ebb to descend upon the sand and to look up and along toward the Leas is to obtain the most characteristic and striking view in the whole place. There, perched up against the sky-line, is the ancient parish church of St. Eanswythe, in modern times frescoed and bedizened and given up to high church practices. There, too, the custom has recently been introduced of going in procession, with cross and vestments, to bless the fishing-nets. One wonders what scornful things Ingoldsby would have said of these doings within the Church of England, and indeed the fishery seems neither better nor worse for them.

FOLKESTONE HARBOUR.

That sainted princess, Eanswythe, daughter of the Kentish King Eadbald, is said to be buried within the church. She was one of the most remarkable of the many wondrous saints of her period, and performed the impossible and brought about the incredible with the best of them. She brought water from Cheriton to Folkestone, making it run up hill, and incompetent carpenters who had sawn beams too short had but to invoke her for them (the beams, not the carpenters) to be

instantly lengthened to any extent desired. Monks, too, it was said, whose cassocks had been washed, and shrunk in the process, could always get them unshrunk in the same marvellous way; but this must be an error of the most flagrant kind, for we know that those holy men washed themselves little, and their clothes never. But whatever marvellous things she could do, she was not capable of the comparatively simple feat of preventing her original conventual church being washed away by the sea.

Folkestone people were of old very largely the butt of the neighbouring towns. They were said to be stupid beyond the ordinary. Twitted on some occasion that has escaped the present historian with not being able to celebrate a given event in poetry, the town produced a poet eager to disprove the accusation. To show what he could do in that way, he took as his theme a notable capture that Folkestone had just then made, and wrote:

> A whale came down the Channel;
> The Dover men could not catch it,
> But the Folkestoners did.

He was, it will be conceded, not even so near an approach to a poet as that mayor who read an address to Queen Elizabeth, beginning with,

> "Most Gracious Queen,
> Welcome to Folkesteen."

to which Her Majesty is said to have replied,

> "You great fool,
> Get off that stool!"

But doubtless these be all malicious inventions. Certainly, though, "great Eliza" did visit Folkestone, and we can have no doubt that the usual address was read—can even see and hear in imagination that mayor reading abysmal ineptitudes "um-um-er-er," like some blundering bumble-bee, the atmosphere growing thick and drowsy with falsities, platitudes, and infinite bombast, until that virginal but vinegary monarch cuts him rudely short. We can see—O! most clear-sighted that we are!—that tall and angular spinster, sharp-visaged, with high, beak-like nose, greatly resembling a gaunt hen—but a very game hen—actually cutting short that turbid flow of mayoral eloquence! we wonder she does not *peck* him.

Still hazardously up and down go those old streets and lanes of the old town

—Beach Street, North Street, Fenchurch Street, Radnor Street, and East Street, whence you look out upon Copt Point and the serried tiers upon tiers of chalk cliffs stretching in the direction of Dover. Still the Martello tower stands upon that point, as it stands in the illustration of Folkestone by Turner, but the swarming population of to-day has blotted out much of that obvious romance that once burst full upon the visitor. The romance is still there, but you have to seek it and dig deep beneath the strata of modern changes before it is found. Trivial things dot the i's, cross the t's, and generally emphasise this triumph of convention. "Lanes" become "streets," and that quaintly illiterate old rendering, "Rendavowe" Street, was long since thought by no means worthy of more educated times, and accordingly changed to the correct spelling of "Rendezvous" it now bears.

Modern Folkestone is already, by effluxion of time, becoming sharply divided into modern and more modern. The ancient Folkestone we have seen to be the fishing village, the first development from whose humble but natural existence, in days when seaside holidays began to be an institution and the "resorts" set out upon their career of artificiality, was the "Pavilionstone" of Dickens and Cubitt. The trail of Cubitt, who built that South Kensington typified by the Cromwell Road, and was followed by his imitators throughout the western suburbs of London in the 'fifties and 'sixties, is all over the land, and is very clearly defined on the Folkestone Leas, whose houses are in the most approved grey stucco style. The Leas therefore are not Folkestone, but, as Dickens dubbed them, "Pavilionstone," or, more justly, Notting-Hill-on-Sea. They and their adjacent contemporary streets are the seaside resort of yesterday; the red-brick and terra-cotta houses and hotels, in adaptation of Elizabethan Gothic and Jacobean Renaissance, that of to-day, a newer and grander place than Cubitt conceived or Dickens knew.

All those magnificent streets, those barrack-like hotels, all those bands and gay parterres, and all the fashion that makes Folkestone the most expensive seaside resort on the south coast, are excrescences. That only is Folkestone where you really do smell the salt water and can seek refuge from the cigar-smoke and the Eau-de-Cologne, the wealthy, the idle, and the vicious, to come to the folk who earn their livelihood by the sea and its fish, and are individual and racy of the water and the always interesting waterside life.

FOLKESTONE IN 1830. *After J. M. W. Turner, R.A.*

The inquirer fails to discover why that hotel, the "Pavilion," of which Dickens was so enamoured, and from whose style and title he named the newly-arising town "Pavilionstone," was given that sign. Napoleon declared, in the course of his great naval works at Cherbourg, that he was resolved to rival the marvels of Egypt; was Cubitt, in his building and contracting way, eager to emulate the plasterous glories of George IV.'s marine palace, the "Pavilion" at Brighton, or, at any rate, to snatch a glamour from its name? The "Pavilion" has been once, certainly—perhaps twice—rebuilt since Dickens wrote, and is now, they say, palatial, and with every circumstance of comfort; but when Pavilionstone was in the making, it seems to have been a sorry sort of a hostelry, in which voyagers for Boulogne had sharp foretastes of the slings and arrows of outrageous fortune which awaited those who resigned themselves to the cross-Channel passage at that period. This, says Dickens, is how you came here for that discomfortable enterprise: "Dropped upon the platform of the main line Pavilionstone Station at eleven o'clock on a dark winter's night, in a roaring wind; and in the howling wilderness outside the station was a short omnibus which brought you up by the forehead the instant you got in at the door; and nobody cared about you, and you were alone in the world. You bumped over infinite chalk until you were turned out at a strange building which had just left off being a barn without having quite begun to be a house, where nobody expected your coming, or knew what to do with you when you were come, and where you were usually blown about until you happened to be blown against the cold beef, and finally into bed. At five in the morning you were blown out of bed, and after a dreary breakfast, with crumpled company, in the midst of confusion, were hustled on board a steamboat, and lay wretched on deck until you saw France lunging and surging at you with great vehemence over the bowsprit."

The miseries of crossing between Folkestone and Boulogne are very greatly assuaged in these times, but still the summer visitants who have exhausted a round of pleasures find a perennial and cruel joy in repairing to the pier, where they can gloat over the miserables who, yellow and green-visaged, step uncertainly ashore after a bad passage.

CHAPTER X

FROM HYTHE TO ASHFORD

From Hythe, where many roads meet, there goes a very picturesque way along the high ground overlooking Romney Marsh—a route intimately associated with "The Leech of Folkestone." It is uphill out of Hythe, of course: indeed, among all the roads out of the town, only the coast routes are flat.

Lympne is the first place on the way—that "Lymme Hill, or Lyme" which Leland says "was sumtyme a famose haven, and good for shyppes that myght cum to the foote of the hille. The place ys yet cawled Shypway and Old Haven."

That it is not now "good for ships" is quite evident to anyone who takes his stand on the cliff-top and views that fifth quarter of the globe, Romney Marsh, from this most eloquent of all view-points. Full three miles away, as the crow flies, the summer wavelets whisper on the beach, and between the margin of the sea and this crumbling cliff-edge, whose foot once dabbled in the waters of the haven, are pastures that have been the anchorage of ships.

Grey buildings of high antiquity rise from the cliff-top and command the mapped-out marshland. The stern tower of Lympne church, forming a beacon for mariners, is next door neighbour to Lympne Castle, once a residence of the Archdeacons of Canterbury. That "castelet embatayled," in the words of Leland is now a farmhouse. Like the church, it was largely built from the stone of the Roman castle down below the cliff; that ancient Portus Lemanis whose feet rested in the waters of the haven and to whose walls the crowding vessels ranged in the grand colonial days of Imperial Rome. Stutsfall Castle the countryfolk call those shattered walls that tell of Roman dominion, rendered "Studfall" on the map.

It is from these crumbling, earthy cliffs of Lympne that one obtains the best and most comprehensive view of Romney Marsh, spread out like an isometric drawing, below. From here the eye ranges over the grey-green levels, until lost in the dim haze of Dungeness, ten miles away. There curves the bay, like the arc of a bended bow, going in a magnificent semicircular sweep into the distance, its margin dotted at regular intervals with those pepper-boxes, the Martello towers, which it was hoped would have made it so hot for Napoleon had he ever descended upon these shores. Nearer at hand—almost, indeed, at our feet—goes the Royal Military Canal, its waters hid from this view-point, but its course defined by the double row of luxuriant trees that clothe its banks. Between foreground and far distance, in a welter of foreshortened fields and hedgerows, lie hid the many hamlets and villages of the marsh. From here it can be seen and felt how open this district is to every breeze that blows, but it needs for the traveller to descend into those levels for him to discover how fiercely the winds lurk behind the contorted hedges of the ridiculously-winding roads, leaping forth at the corners and seizing one with the rude grip of a strong man. Save for the direct road that leads from Hythe to Dymchurch and New Romney, and that other from thence to Snargate and Appledore, the marshland ways are mazy and deceptive, impassable ditches and drains rendering likely-looking short cuts impracticable. To approach a place coyly, and as though really going away from it, is the road method of Romney Marsh, and to strike boldly in the direction of any given spot is to make tolerably sure of never reaching it. Thus, when the stranger with dismay perceives the distant village for which he has been setting forth slipping by degrees behind him, he should know that he is on the right road, but when he observes its church tower towering straight ahead, then let him pause and anxiously inquire the way. When these facts are borne in mind there will be little wonder that Romney Marsh was among the last strongholds of superstition and smuggling.

ROMNEY MARSH, FROM LYMPNE.

The last smuggler has long since died, less in the odour of sanctity than of unexcised schnapps, and not since sixty years ago has a witch been credibly reported, sailing athwart the moon on a besom. Now, when cattle fall victims to the ills common to them, instead of "swimming" the nearest half-daft and wholly ill-favoured old woman, the farmers send to Hythe or Ashford for a veterinary surgeon.

It is a romantic view-point, this outlook from Lympne cliff, and quite unspoiled. You can have it wholly to yourself the livelong day, except for the occasional passage of a farm-hand, whose natural avocations take him past. It has not become a show-place and, by consequence, self-conscious. A steep and rough undercliff, a tangled mass of undergrowth clinging to the cliff itself, a cottage nestling beneath, and church and castle stark against the sky-line—that is Lympne from below. The purest of water spouts from the cliff-face, from a pipe—the shrunken representative of the river Limen—and landsprings give the fields a perennial verdure.

LYMPNE CASTLE.

Lympne, despite its weird spelling, is merely "Lim"; how or why the "p" got into the place-name is unknown. The village—a small and drowsy one—describes a semicircle enclosing the church and its neighbour, and though pretty, is not in any way remarkable, save that it has an inn oddly named the "County Members," and a cottage bearing the quaintly pretty tablet pictured on the next page. The church is a grim stern church, exactly suited to its situation, with massive Early Norman and Early English interior, disdainful of ornament. The heavy door of the north porch is boldly patterned in nails, "A. G. C. W. 1708."

A COTTAGE TABLET, LYMPNE.

It is a Roman road that runs along the cliff-top through Lympne to Aldington, passing the hamlet of Court-at-Street that was once the Roman "Belerica," and emerging upon the "open plain" of Aldington Frith. "Allington Fright" as the Kentish peasantry name it, is still an open expanse. The airs of romance blow freely about it to-day, as of old, and although from the high ground by Aldington Forehead distant glimpses of Hythe and its big neighbour, Folkestone, whether you desire it or not, are obtained, the place is solitary, and the country, still unspoiled, dips down southward to "The Mesh" and the sea, over crumbling earthy cliffs, tangled with impenetrable bracken, blackberry brambles, and hazel coppices. This is the especial district of that fine prose legend, "The Leech of Folkestone"—"Mrs. Botherby's Story," as Ingoldsby names it. The place has ever been the home of superstition and the miraculous. To quote Ingoldsby himself, "Here it was, in the neighbouring chapelry, the site of which may yet be traced by the curious antiquary, that Elizabeth Barton, the 'Holy Maid of Kent,' had commenced that series of supernatural pranks which eventually procured for her head an unenvied elevation upon London Bridge." Although that eminent pluralist and cautious though fiery reformer, Erasmus, was Rector of Aldington in 1511, and opposed, alike by policy and temperament, to shams and spiritual trickery, the old leaven of superstition worked freely in his time, and, indeed, survived until recent years. Nay, more than that, these solitudes still harbour beliefs in the uncanny. The district, as of old, has an ill name, and the warlocks and other unholy subjects of Satan, once reported to make its wild recesses their favourite rendezvous, are found even now, in confidential interludes, to be not wholly vanished from the rural imagination. The moralist, from his lofty pinnacle, of course condemns these darkling survivals, but there be those, not so committed to matter-of-fact, who, revolting from the obvious and the commonplace, welcome the surviving folklore, and, plunging into its haunts, forget awhile the fashion of Folkestone, Sandgate, and Hythe.

A KENTISH FARM.

The allusion in "The Leech of Folkestone" to the "neighbouring chapelry" is a reference to an ancient chapel of Our Lady whose roofless walls are still to be found on the undercliff at the roadside hamlet of Court-at-Street, situated on a little unobtrusive plateau midway between the level of the road from Hythe to Aldington and the drop to Romney Marsh. This, in those old days, was one of those minor places of pilgrimage which, possessing only an inferior collection of relics and being situated in out-of-the-way nooks and corners, could not command the crowds and the rich offerings common at such shrines as those of St. Thomas á Becket, and other saints of his calibre. It is, indeed, a shy and retiring place, and the stranger not in search of it and not careful to make minute inquiries would most certainly miss the spot. It is gained down a short steep trackway beside the Court Lodge Farm, and, when found, forms a pleasing and unconventional peep—the delight of the artist, and at the same time his despair, because he cannot hope to convey into his sketch that last accent of romance the place owns. Here, where the track dips down and becomes a hollow way, the great gnarled roots of the thickly-clustering trees are seen in their lifelong desperate clutch at the powdering soil, and the trunks, wreathed here and there with ivy, shouldering one another in their competition for light and sustenance, form a heavy and massive frame to the picture beyond—a picture of ruined chapel and sullen pool, fed by landsprings from the broken cliff, and level marsh beyond, bounded only by that insistent row of Martello towers, and by the dull silver of the sea.

THE RUINED CHAPEL, COURT-AT-STREET.

The story of the "Holy Maid of Kent" is intimately connected with this chapel. It seems that in 1525 there was living at the cottage still standing at Aldington, and called "Cobb's Hall," one Thomas Cobb, bailiff to my Lord

Archbishop of Canterbury, who, among his many other fat manors, owned all this expanse of Aldington, then largely a hunting forest. We do not know much of Thomas Cobb, but of his servant-maid, Elizabeth Barton, we possess a fund of information, now humorous and then tragical. Like Joan of Arc, Elizabeth Barton was quite a humble and uneducated peasant-girl. Her very name is rustic, "barton" being a term even now in use to denote a barn or cattle-shed. In midst of her service at "Cobb's Hall" this poor Elizabeth is stricken down by an extraordinary complication of internal bodily disease and mental affliction.

Alas! poor Elizabeth—no longer shall you scour pots or cleanse plates; no more for you are the homely domestic duties of the bailiff's home!

OLD SUNDIAL, ALDINGTON.

Wasted by sufferings that all the arts of the purblind medical practitioners of that time could not assuage, those doctors declared that there was something more than ordinary in her affliction. Some merely thought their science not sufficient for a cure; others, anxious for the professional credit of themselves and the practice of medicine, darkly hinted that here was an instance of demoniacal possession; and others yet, listening to the half-conscious ravings of the unhappy girl, took another view, and, devoutly crossing themselves, averred that this was a visitation from God, and that she was becoming possessed of a divine knowledge of things to be. A perusal of the quaint and voluminous contemporary records of Elizabeth Barton's career disposes one to the belief that her ailments brought on a condition of temporary, but recurrent, religious mania. She had always been a devout girl, as the parish priest, Richard Masters, was ready to declare; but neither he, nor any of his time, knew anything of mania of the religious variety, and when, called to her bedside, he saw and heard her in trances and somnambulistic excursions, implicitly believed that the "very godly certain things concerning the seven deadly sins and the Ten Commandments" she was heard to narrate were inspired. Those who had believed her demoniacally possessed were refuted by these pious sayings. The Devil, it was obvious, had no part in these things, but the Holy Ghost was working, through the medium of this poor peasant girl, to great events.

That was a time when such manifestations were, from the point of view of the Church, eminently desirable. Reformation was knocking at the gates of Popery—thunderous knocks and not to be denied. The Roman Catholic clergy and their religion were fast becoming discredited, and it was necessary to bolster up it and them by any means. The story of Joan of Arc, although a hundred years old, was by no means forgotten, and it was thought that what the farm-maiden of Domrémy could do for the Crown of France, this native product of Kentish soil might achieve for the Catholic Church in England.

So Richard Masters, enthusiastic, took horse and rode all the way from Aldington to Lambeth Palace, where the old and doting Archbishop Warham, in fear and rage at the impious dealings of Henry VIII. with Holy Church, received the story of this Kentish miracle with a hope that something might come of it. A good deal actually did so come, but not greatly to the advantage of Roman Catholicism.

"Keep you," said he, "diligent accompt of all her utterances: they come surely of God, and tell her that she is not to refuse or hide His goodness and works."

As a result of this ghostly advice of the Archbishop, Masters returned and persuaded Bailiff Cobb that pot-scouring and scullery-work were occupations distinctly beneath the dignity of one clearly the elect of the Holy Spirit, and she was promoted immediately to the place of an honoured guest in his house. At the same time she experienced a recovery, and became again the clumsy, big-footed country wench of yore. Meanwhile, however, the fame of her "prophecies" was bruited about in all that countryside—the cunning Richard Masters saw to that—and Cobb's house became a place of pilgrimage. Some came for the merely vulgar purpose of having their fortunes told; others sought the laying on of hands, for one so gifted could surely cure the ailing; and all combined to make Cobb's life a misery.

None was more disappointed at her recovery and consequent descent from supernatural heights to her former commonplace level than Elizabeth herself, and she determined to simulate her former natural trances. This iniquity seems to have been suggested by the Church, in the persons of two monks sent by the Archbishop from Canterbury. Those worthies, the cellarer of the Priory of Christ Church, one Doctor Bocking, and Dan William Hadley—took her under instruction. They educated the previously ignorant girl in the marvellous legends of the old Catholic female saints, taught her to believe herself one of that company, and coached her in all the abstruse doctrines of their religion. In her recurring cataleptic states, sometimes real, but oftener feigned, she re-delivered all these doctrines, and naturally astonished those who had known her for ignorant and absolutely without education, into a belief in her divine mission.

ALDINGTON.

At this juncture it was thought desirable to transfer her to the neighbouring Chapel of Our Lady, where she might not only work good to the Church in general, but attract pilgrims and their offerings to the shrine, which of late had been doing very bad business, and was scarcely self-supporting. No one in our own times understands the art of advertisement better than did the religious of those days, and the occasion of her transference from Cobb's Hall to the Chapel was made the occasion for a great ceremonial. She had given out that she "would never take health of her body till such time as she had visited the image of Our Lady" at that place, and, indeed, declared that the Virgin had appeared to her and promised recovery on her obedience.

On that great day—the thing had been made so public—there were over two thousand persons present to witness the promised miracle, the whole concourse singing the Litany and repeating psalms and orations while Elizabeth was borne to the spot on a litter, acting to perfection the part of one possessed, "her face wondrously disfigured, her tongue hanging out, and her eyes being in a manner plucked out and lying upon her cheeks. There was then heard a voice speaking within her belly, as it had been in a tunne, her lips not greatly moving; she all that while continuing by the space of three hours or more in a trance. The which voice, when it told anything of the joys of

Heaven, spake so sweetly and so heavenly that every man was ravished with the hearing thereof; and contrarywise, when it told anything of Hell, it spake so horribly and terribly that it put the hearers in a great fear. It spake also many things for the confirmation of pilgrimages and trentals, hearing of masses and confession, and many other such things. And after she had lyen there a long time, she came to herself again, and was perfectly whole"; and no wonder, for she was shamming all the while, with the aid of a cunning ventriloquist, who thus spoke so sweetly of Heaven and so horribly of Hell.

But this "miracle" so successfully imposed upon the people that she was, without exception, regarded as a saint. The Virgin, on second thoughts, personally desired her not to take up her residence in the Chapel, but to take Dr. Bocking for her spiritual father, to assume the name of Sister Elizabeth, and to proceed to the Priory of St. Sepulchre, in Canterbury. The blasphemies easy to the Catholics of that time could not possibly be better shown than by this narration.

Her progress of impudent imposture at Canterbury is more than surprising—it astounds the inquirer. She delivered oracles, which were printed and commanded a large sale, and to her, for advice on the religious questions then agitating the realm, resorted many of the noblest and best in the land. Of course, with the tuition and under the protection of the Church, her opinions and advice were distinctly against the King, whom she grew so rash as to threaten, on the question of his divorce and re-marriage. Nay, more, she found it possible to admonish the Pope. Sir Thomas More believed in her holy mission; Catherine of Aragon, the divorced Queen, supported her; Henry alone cared not a rap for her prophecies of disaster. She actually forced a way into his presence at Canterbury, on his return from France. He should not, she declared, reign a month after he married Anne Boleyn, and "should die a villain's death"; but he married her—and nothing happened. Strange to say—strange, after all we have heard of Henry's ferocity—nothing either happened at that time to the "Holy Maid" herself. She postponed the date of the coming disaster—put it forward a month—and still nothing happened. Greatly to the surprise of many, the King still reigned and seemed happy enough.

Meanwhile the most extravagant claims were made for the "Holy Maid." Once every fortnight, from the chapel in the Priory, she was, amidst celestial melodies, taken up to Heaven, to God and the saints. Her passage to the chapel lay through the monks' dormitory, and, according to the acts of accusation levelled against her, her pilgrimages to that chapel were not altogether so innocent of carnal things as could have been desired. Angels constantly visited her in her cell, and when they had departed came the Devil himself, horned, hoofed, and breathing sulphureous fumes, in manner appropriate. Accounts the monks gave of this last visitor were, however, not always received with that respectful belief anticipated, and so the Maid submitted to a hole being burnt in her hand, to convince the incredulous that Old Nick had come and attempted her virtue. It is impossible to quote the grossly indecent monkish stories; but they are ingenious, as also was their practice of escorting pilgrims to the outside of her cell when the Evil One was supposed to be present. The visitors observed with their own physical eyes, and smelt, with their own nostrils, the "great stinking smokes, savouring grievously," that then issued from the crevices of the door; and went away, fearing greatly. Later, when she was arrested, a stock of brimstone and assafœtida was discovered in her apartment, and these diabolical stinks found ready explanation.

She ran a course of three years' blasphemous deception before the Act of Attainder was prepared, under which she and several of her accomplices were arrested, found guilty of high treason, and executed at Tyburn. That same Richard Masters who discovered her existence to the religious world, Dr. Bocking and four others suffered with her, on April 21st, 1534. Her last words have their own interest. "Hither," said she, addressing the people, "I am come to die. I have been not only the cause of mine own death, which most justly I have deserved, but am also the cause of the death of all these persons which at this time here suffer. And yet I am not so much to be blamed, considering that it was well known unto these learned men that I was a poor wench without learning; and therefore they might have easily perceived that the things which were done by me could not proceed in no such sort; but their capacities and learning could right well judge that they were altogether feigned. But because the things which I feigned were profitable unto them, therefore they much praised me, and bare me in hand that it was the Holy Ghost, and not I that did them. And I, being puffed up with their praises, fell into a proud and foolish fantasye with myself, and thought I might feign what I would, which thing hath brought me to this case, and for the which I now cry to God and the King's Highness most heartily mercy, and desire all you good people to pray to God to have mercy on me, and all them that here suffer with me."

"If," says Lambarde, who was amused by the Maid's impudent career—"if these companions could have let the King of the land alone, they might have plaied their pageants as freely as others have been permitted, howsoever it tended to the dishonour of the King of Heaven."

CHAPTER XI

FROM HYTHE TO ASHFORD (*continued*)

COBB'S HALL.

"Cobb's Hall" stands prominently to the left of the road, after passing by the village of Aldington, and is a very noticeable old half-timbered rustic dwelling-house, now interiorly divided into two cottages. In the upstairs bedroom of one may be seen the remains of a fine decorative plaster ceiling and a strange pictorial plaster frieze surmounting a blocked-up fireplace. This singular design is old enough to have been here in Elizabeth Barton's time, and she must have been familiar with its representations of Adam and Eve and their highly problematical surroundings of queer birds and beasts, not modelled from the life, and now, after centuries of wear and many coats of paint, so blunted and battered that it is difficult to tell certainly whether any particular plaster protuberance is intended for an elephant, a sheep, or a crow.

ALDINGTON KNOLL.

BILSINGTON WOODS.

To the left of Aldington, on a road through the alder thickets, hugging the edge of the cliffs, is Aldington Knoll, a very remarkable hillock rising boldly and bare from above the surrounding brushwood and coppices. In the legend of "The Leech of Folkestone" it is described as "a sort of woody promontory, in shape almost conical, its sides covered with thick underwood, above which is seen a bare and brown summit, rising like an Alp in miniature." To this spot it was that Master Marsh resorted, at the rising of the moon, for his meeting with the conjuror, Aldrovando. Barham well chose this legendary Knoll of Aldington for that miraculous *séance*, for this is not only a well-known landmark, but is the subject of much folklore. Thus, the older rustics will tell how the Knoll is said to be guarded by drowned sailors, keeping watch and ward over a gigantic skeleton with a great sword, unearthed "once upon a time" by a reckless digger for the treasure once popularly supposed to be buried here. Something very terrible happened to that unfortunate spadesman, and since then a general consensus of rustic opinion has left the Knoll alone. A local rhyme tells how—

> Where he dug the chark shone white
> To sea, like Calais Light;

but that is poetic license, the prehistoric barrow—for such it seems to be— that crests the Knoll is of yellow sand and gravel.

BILSINGTON PRIORY.

Beyond, in a tract of country thickly covered with scrubwood, is the village of Bilsington, with Bilsington Priory, now a farmhouse, standing remote in midst of eight hundred acres of copse. It is a grimly picturesque house, this desecrated Priory of St. Augustine, and doubly haunted—firstly by a prior who tells red-hot beads, and secondly by the spook of a woman who was murdered by her husband for accidentally smashing a trayfull of china. The nightly crashings are said by the most unveracious witnesses to still continue, but however that may be, the place certainly is haunted by innumerable owls, who roost fearlessly in some of the deserted rooms.

Away by the roadside is Bilsington village, its moated Court Lodge Farm and parish church grouped together. It was Bilsington bell that struck *One!* in "The Leech of Folkestone," and advised Master Marsh that his torments were, for the time, over.

BILSINGTON CHURCH.

By Ruckinge and Ham Street we come up Orlestone Hill, that "Quaker-coloured ravine" described in the story of "Jerry Jarvis's Wig." "The road," says Ingoldsby, "had been cut deep below the surface of the soil, for the purpose of diminishing the abruptness of the descent, and as either side of the superincumbent banks was clothed with a thick mantle of tangled copsewood, the passage, even by day, was sufficiently obscure, the level beams of the rising or setting sun, as they happened to enfilade the gorge, alone illuminating its recesses."

The cutting is there to this day, but it must be confessed that neither it nor the hill are so steep as that description would have us believe. Here it was that the body of Humphry Bourne was found, murdered by Joe Washford, demoniacally possessed and incited by the wig that Jerry Jarvis, the scoundrelly solicitor of Appledore, had given him.

ORLESTONE HILL.

From the little church of Orlestone that, with a picturesque black and white manor house crowns the hill, it is five miles into the market-town, and railway centre of Ashford.

CHAPTER XII

THE BACK OF BEYOND: THE HINTERLAND OF FOLKESTONE AND HYTHE

The business of getting out of Folkestone is a weariful affair, for there are not only the heavy rises in the roads to be surmounted, but the great rolling chalk hills that shut in the valleys reverberate the heat of the sun to a degree that is often stifling, and in these latter days the tiresome hindmost suburbs of Folkestone conspire to render the explorer's lot a hard one, going back dustily inland, beyond Radnor Park, until they join forces with what was once the rural village of Cheriton Street.

It is a remarkable stretch of country to which one comes at last; a tumbled area of bare, grassy chalk downs, rising up into bold sugarloaf peaks and cones, very dry and parching. Shorncliffe Camp is hard by, occupying the high ground between Cheriton and Sandgate, and up and down this valley and these hillsides it is the fate of the brave defenders of their country to be manœuvred, in season and out. When the soldiers of Shorncliffe Camp look down from their windy eyrie upon the long, dry course of the valley, they feel tired and thirsty, and as they look on it every day this amounts to saying that the thirst of Shorncliffe Camp is a transcendent thirst, and not to be measured by ordinary standards. The sweating swaddy's acute thirst is induced by reminiscent and prospective agonies of drought in the reviews and field-days, past and to come, in that waterless bottom.

He and his forebears have been learning their martial trade here for considerably over a hundred years, for it was in 1794 that Shorncliffe Camp was first founded, to house the despondent and ragged troops landed from the disastrous retreat of Sir John Moore upon Corunna. They learn their drill with every circumstance of unmilitary squalor and untidiness at Shorncliffe, and although they are turned out with pomp and display on grand occasions, the dirt and raggedness of the camp itself, and the makeshift out-at-elbows appearance of men and material, do not form a picture of military glory. Tommy "at home" at Shorncliffe is a very different creature from the oiled and curled darling of the nursemaids on the sea-front at Hythe or Seabrook; and with unshaven face, short pipe in mouth, in shirt-sleeves and with braces dangling about his legs, wandering among the domestic refuse and garbage that plentifully bestrew the place, looks very little like a hero.

It is very pleasant to leave the struggling shops of the ultimate Folkestone suburbs behind, to forget the strenuous struggles with bankruptcy waged by those pioneer shopkeepers at the Back of Beyond, and to bid good-bye at length to the last outposts of the pavements, the kerbstones, and the lamp-standards. It is not, however, so pleasing, having put all these evidences of civilisation behind one, to observe, peering over the distant hillside, a vast building which on inquiry proves to be the workhouse, another, and a rather grim, reminder of that civilisation which in one extremity flaunts in silks and satins on the Folkestone Leas, and in the other sets its servants, the ministrants to all that display, to eke out an objectless existence in stuff and corduroy within this giant barrack. It is the dark reverse of the bright picture of south coast life and fashion.

It is a relief to turn away from this evidence of Folkestone's prosperity, and to secure a quiet hillside nook whence, on one of those insufferably hot days invariably selected for elaborate evolutions and parades, to watch the sweating Tommies harried up and down the blistering valley in the service of their country, to the raucous and unintelligible yells of commanding officers, comfortably and coolly supervising their heated efforts from the easeful vantage-point of horseback. The contemplative pilgrim finds the energy thus displayed by rank and file to be what a tradesman would call "splendid value" for the reward of a shilling a day, but dolefully admits to himself that not for less than four times that pay can he obtain a man to do a job of honest, but less laborious and exacting, work in a private capacity.

Up yonder, on the hillside, the signallers are working the heliograph and energetically waving flags. Their energy makes one positively feel tired. It is "Cæsar's Camp" whence the bright dot-and-dash signal-flashes of the heliograph are proceeding; if we were clever enough, or duly trained, we could read the messages sent. We must not suppose, because "Cæsar's Camp" is so named, that Cæsar himself, or any other Roman, ever camped there: if he had camped in half the places so called, he would have had no time for fighting. Julius Cæsar, in fact, is said to have camped, and Queen Elizabeth to have slept, in more places than their poor ghosts would recognise if they were ever allowed to revisit these glimpses of the moon. Nay, even in "regions Cæsar never knew" his camps absurdly appear. It is quite certain, for example, that the great general was never in South Africa, and yet "Cæsar's Camp," overlooking Ladysmith, was the scene of much fighting in the second Boer War.

A complete change from this scene of martial glory and perspiration is Cheriton itself, where the ancient church stands on a hilltop, away from Cheriton Street. In the rear go the chasing lights and shades of sun and clouds, racing over the yellow-green of the grassy hills; ahead plunges a tree-shaded winding line leading unexpectedly to the sea. It is the one unspoiled little rural oasis in the urban and suburban deserts of a seaboard that has grown fashionable. All too soon it ends, and the villas of Seabrook are reached.

Seabrook and Hythe we have already seen. Now let us strike boldly inland, and, leaving Hythe to the left, tackle the perpetual rise and fall of the roads that lead past the romantic castle of Saltwood to the bosky glades of Westenhanger.

SALTWOOD CASTLE.

Saltwood Castle is a peculiarly interesting object in the Ingoldsby Country, for it was the place where the four knights who murdered Becket assembled, on the night before the tragedy, and FitzUrse, among them, was, as we have already seen, claimed by Barham as his ancestor. The massive circular stone entrance-towers of the Castle come into view as we turn inland and surmount the crest of the hill at the back of Hythe. From this hilltop it is seen how exquisitely beautiful was the situation of Saltwood in days of old, before Hythe and its neighbouring mushroom townlets had begun to throw out their villas and suburban residences upon the spurs of the downs, flouting the sylvan solitude and mediæval aloofness of that secluded fortress. It lies a mile inland, at the head of a green and moist valley, still thickly wooded, sloping to the sea. We do not fully realise, until we take thought, the due meaning of that beautiful name of Saltwood; but, dwelling upon its old history, and in imagination sweeping away the modern accretions of houses, it is possible to recover the look of that Saltwood of old, when the woodlands were even more dense than now, and extended to the very margin of the sea; when a little pebbly brook came prattling from the bosom of the downs beyond, and, overhung by forest trees, found its way to the beach. The high tides then oozed some little distance up the valley, and the trees dipped their branches in the mingled waters of sea and stream. No roads, save the merest bridle-paths, then led up to the Castle, whose towers rose from amid the encircling trees like some fortress of fairyland.

From very early times Saltwood Castle was held by the Archbishops of Canterbury. It was, indeed, the seizure of this archiepiscopal castle and demesne by the Crown, and the grant of them to Randulf de Broc, that formed one of Becket's bitter grievances against Henry II. De Broc and his relatives were not only seated on the Archbishop's property, but were given the custody of his palace at Canterbury during his long six years' banishment, and on his return in December 1170, strenuously set themselves to be as insolent and as injurious as possible. Randulf himself hunted down the Archbishop's deer with the Archbishop's own hounds, and seized a vessel off Hythe laden with wine, a present from the King to Becket, killing some of the crew and casting the survivors into the dungeons of Pevensey. It was ill business quarrelling with that heady family, unanimously bent upon spiting and spoiling his Grace, from bloody murder and the seizing and destroying of property down to acts of wanton and provocative petty buffoonery. While Randulf de Broc was committing murder and piracy upon the high seas, his kinsman Robert, a renegade monk, on Christmas Eve waylaid one of the Archbishop's sumpter-mules and one of his horses and cut off their tails. It was this minor indignity that made the greater impression upon Becket's mind. For it he cursed and excommunicated both Randulf and Robert on Christmas Day from the nave pulpit of Canterbury Cathedral.

Saltwood Castle, however, and the De Brocs bore a still further part in the tragedy of Becket, now fast drawing to its final act. When the four knights, Reginald FitzUrse, Hugh de Moreville, William de Tracy, and Richard le Bret, rushed forth from the King's presence at his court of Bur, in Normandy, on the night of December 24th, with murder in their hearts, they agreed to cross the Channel by two different routes, landing at Dover and at Winchelsea and meeting here, in this fortalice of Saltwood, where hatred sat embattled, already excommunicated and given over in any case to damnation, and so ready for any deed. Ghastly legends, theatrical in the rich gloom of their staging, tell how the four from over sea and Randulf de Broc met here, and plotted together on this night of December 28th the deed that was to be done on the morrow; arranging all the details of that act of blood in the dark, with extinguished candles, fearful of seeing each other's faces—so strong a hold did the event take of the popular imagination. The next morning, calling together a troop of soldiers in the King's name, they galloped off to Canterbury, along the Stone Street, to the commission of that crime whose echoes have come down to us, still hoarsely reverberant, despite the passing of more than seven centuries.

But it must not be supposed that here at Saltwood we see the veritable walls that sheltered those assassins. There is nothing remaining at Saltwood that can take us back to the days of Becket. The oldest, as well as the most imposing, part is the entrance, whose great drum-towers, built or restored by the cruel and haughty Archbishop Courtenay about 1350, give a very striking impression to one who stands beneath them of the almost impregnable strength of such mediæval strongholds before the days of heavy ordnance— the walls are so thick and smooth, the loophole windows so high up and small, the stout gate so strengthened with iron. If to force such a place seems almost impossible in cold blood, what of the time when it was defended by determined persons who heaved heavy stones from the battlements, so high up, upon the devoted heads of the equally determined persons, so far below; when the molten lead poured down in silvery cascades, to burn through the flesh to the very bone, and the winged missiles sped from the arbalasts into the liver of many a gallant warrior?—

> The oak door is heavy and brown;
>> And with iron it is plated and machicollated,
> To pour boiling oil and lead down;
>> How you'd frown
> Should a ladle-full fall on your crown!

One is altogether indisposed to quarrel with the very thoroughgoing restoration that has given these great entrance-towers so striking an air of newness, for one instinctively feels that these towers must have looked so in times when the garrison was still kept up. While the place remained a fortress-residence it would have been simply suicidal not to maintain the entrance in the utmost state of repair.

The arms of Courtenay—the three-pointed label and the three bezants—supported by an angel, still remain over the entrance, but Courtenay himself, before whose frown his unfortunate tenants trembled, and in whose rare and uncertain smiles they dared to breathe in deprecating fashion, is forgotten locally. In Cornwall, in Wales, or in any Celtic part of Great Britain he would have survived in wild diabolic legend, but in Kent, which has been phlegmatic and matter-of-fact ever since Hengist and Horsa and the rest of the Teutons landed, he has long been consigned to dryasdust records, where his memory lingers, inanimate. When a little of the dust has been banged out of him, he can be made to strut the stage again and lord it once more, like the very full-blooded tyrant he was, zealous in upholding the spiritualities and the temporalities of the Church, and fanatic in the exaction of deference and manorial dues to himself. Did any poor hind or woodsman offend, ever so unconsciously, in failing of that deference, why, let him be seized and flung into some Little Ease or earthly purgatory, damply underground, there to reflect, with stripes, upon the majesty of Archbishops in general, and of Courtenays in particular, and to wonder when it shall please my lord to release him. Meanwhile, his Grace has forgotten all about his victim, and is thundering in his manorial court against the trembling bailiffs and townsfolk of his manor of Hythe, who have not done him, as he imagines, that yeoman service which is his due, and have now come to compound for that dereliction with fines in good coin and propitiatory offerings for his table, such as porpoises (the old records call them "porpusses") and others of the beastly dishes that mediæval times delighted in. All these folk had cause to rejoice when his exacting Grace died in 1396, and made way for a milder occupant of the seat of St. Augustine, but they were not happy until the Reformation came and the Church and the manor parted company. The property now belongs to the Deedes family, but it needs no very prophetic eye to discern the ultimate fate of Saltwood's ownership. It lies too near the gates of the consorted towns of Hythe and Folkestone and their satellites to be much longer suffered to maintain its present semi-solitude, and the day will come when it and its romantic setting of woods will be offered to and purchased by those towns as a public park. The landscape-gardener will be let loose upon it; winding gravel paths of the kind that takes a league of path to go a mile of distance will be made, and the public will be requested to "keep off the grass" and to "place all refuse in the receptacle provided for the purpose": all very parlourmaidenly, and the essence of neatness and order, but—well, there! one can imagine the choleric ghosts of De Broc and Courtenay and those of many a gross man-at-arms or warlike seneschal walking on the grass in derision, or with ineffective kicks of impalpable mailed feet seeking to demolish the receptacles.

Magnificently-wooded hills stretch from Saltwood inland to Westenhanger, and the delightful road goes full in view of the gorgeous sylvan beauties of Sandling Park, presently to come to a broad highway running due north and south, beside whose straight course the ruined, ivy-clad outworks and towers of an ancient mansion are seen, in whose midst is planted an eighteenth-century mansion. This is Westenhanger House, erected by Squire Champneys in place of that older manor house which was built on the site of a still more ancient fortified place by Henry VIII. Like many another manor of ancient descent, Westenhanger has been many times in and out of Royal possession. Its odd name, inviting inquiry, really means no more than, in modern parlance, "Westwood," and is derived from the Saxon *angra*. It is mentioned in a deed of St. Augustine's monastery as "Le Hangre," and was early divided into two portions, Westen and Osten (or eastern) Hanger. Remains of the moat that once surrounded the old fortified mansion are still to be seen, together with the defensible towers.

WESTENHANGER HOUSE.

Westenhanger stands upon the old Stone Street from Lympne to Canterbury, surrounded by densely wooded parks and neighboured unromantically in these times by a railway—nay, more, a railway junction. One might suppose that the force of modernity could no further go, but that supposition would be an error, for the grounds of the famous old place have been of late years converted into a racecourse, and Westenhanger House itself is given up to the business of a new turf enterprise—a sufficiently thorough change from those remote times when it was a bower of Henry II. and the Fair Rosamond, that beauteous harlot of whom Queen Eleanor was so very properly jealous, and for whose safety from the queenly nails and tongue the infatuated king built several artful retreats in various parts of the country. The chief bower of the wanton Rosamond was at Woodstock. Its like, according to the old ballad-writers, was never seen. It had a hundred and fifty doors, and a vast number of secret passages, so cunningly contrived that no one could find a way in or out without the aid of a thread. Despite those precautions, or possibly because there were a hundred and forty-nine doors too many, the furious Queen Eleanor *did* enter and poisoned the "Rosa Mundi"; and "a good job, too," will be the verdict of most people with properly-developed domestic instincts. Rosamond was buried in all the unmerited pomp and odour of sanctity in Godstow Nunnery. If that shameless young person had remained at Westenhanger, where there was, apparently not so embarrassing a choice of doors, she might have escaped the Queen's vengeance altogether. Nothing, however, at Westenhanger is of so great an age as Rosamond's day, although, to be sure, the remaining angle-towers were built only some forty years later.

Stone Street, that goes so broad and straight on towards Canterbury, is not the deserted road that many are inclined to think it. Once a week it is populated by a stream of carriers' covered carts going between Canterbury and the obscure villages on either side of the Roman way, not yet within touch of railways; and some very quaint survivals are to be found on those occasions.

There are carriers from sleepy hollows who are as russet in complexion and clothing from head to foot as the soil, and as much a product of it as the trees and fruits. These are those true Kentish men in whose mouths the sound of "th" is impossible, and who pronounce the definite article "the" like a Frenchman. To hear a Kentish rustic holding forth upon the iniquities of "de wedder" when he is intent upon abusing the climate is as humorous an interlude as to listen to a Kentish housewife who talks in unaccustomed plurals and asks the hungry tourist at tea if he will have any more "bread and butters."

Others there are in a way less rustic, if equally provincial. These are those grand seigneurs in the carrying line who sport ancient silk or beaver hats and wear broadcloth of an antique cut—broadcloth that was once black and hats that of old were glossy. If the clothes can scarcely be suspected of being heirlooms, the hats certainly are. They are extremely rare and genuine stove-pipes, calculated to impress the rural neighbours with the dignity of the wearers and to extinguish the casual stranger at Canterbury with spasms of laughter. "He were giv' me by my feyder," said Carrier Hogben of Postling, who, alas, is now gathered to his kin in the rural churchyard; and that amazing headgear seemed to gather respect to itself when referred to in the masculine gender. It seemed to stand more upright, and to look more rigid, if that were possible. "Yes," he repeated, "m' feyder givvimee, and 'e's still a good 'un. Dey don't mek 'at's like 'e now," he added with pride, as he carefully brushed it the wrong way with his coat-sleeve, so that the nap stood up like the fur of a cat when it sees a strange dog. One used to heartily agree that hats of that sort are *not* made nowadays. Hogben was then wont to give a grunt of satisfaction. "Cloes used to be made to *last*," he would say, as he carefully replaced that gruesome tile in the box that had held it close upon forty years, "and folks when dey'd got a good 'at, took care of 'im."

Having put away that impressive head-covering and resumed his everyday clothes, "Mr. Jeremiah Hogben," as he was respectfully known by his rustic neighbours on carrying days and Sundays, became simple "old Jerry" or "old Hogben" for the rest of the week. It was as though a king had relinquished his robes and regalia and come among the people as one of themselves.

Mr. Hogben, in common with the rest of the countryside, had a good deal of inaccurate lore respecting the Stone Street. According to him, it was made by the builders of Canterbury Cathedral, to convey stone quarried at Lympne to the scene of operations. He declined to believe in the Romans. They were "foreigners," and as such, incapable of road-making—"or anything else," as he sweepingly declared. Mr. Hogben had seen a foreigner once: an Italian with a monkey and a hurdy-gurdy organ, who had found his way to Postling by mistake—the only manner in which strangers ever do find themselves in that village. Not having been present at this rencounter, it is difficult to determine which of the trio was the more astonished—the monkey, the Italian, or Mr. Hogben. Presumably the monkey, for at sight of the carrier and his hat the terrified animal escaped up a tree, whence his master only recovered him after much trouble and many "Per Baccos!" "Swearing awful, he was," according to Hogben.

"Do you understand Italian, then?" we asked.

"Lor' bless ye, no, sir; whatever put dat in yer 'ed: no Eyetalian for me, so long as I can talk Inglish; and when dey tells me dat such as dem, mid deir monkeys and orgins, made this ere roäd what we're travelling on, why, I begs to not believe a bit of it."

"But the modern Italians and the ancient Romans are not precisely the same people."

"So gentlemen like you've told me afore; but what I says is, dey both comes from Italy, don't dey? Well den, it stands to reason dey're the same. No people what goes about the country playing hurdy-gurdies ever made this roäd, I'll stake me life on't."

If Hogben had no respect for foreigners, his manner indicated that he owned an awed kind of deference to the memory of Lord Rokeby of Mount Morris, past which park he had driven on his way to and from Canterbury for many years. Which of the several Barons Rokeby it was whose doings in lifetime and whose post-mortem pranks were the theme of his discourses, does not appear. "He had a goolden bart" (he meant "bath") "for Sundays and a marble one for week-days, and he'd sit in 'em all de marciful day long and read de papers and have his bit o' grub. When he got tired o' dat, and t'ought he'd like a stroll, he'd just nip outer de bart and walk about de park, as naked as Adam before dey inwented fig-leaves. An' now" (? cause and effect) "he drives down de Stone Street every midnight, wid his head in his lap and four coal-black haases, breading fire. No, I can't say I ever seed him—and dunnosiwanto: reckon I'd run awaiy. I knewed a man what *did* see 'im, and it gran' nigh druv 'im off n 'is 'ed."

Such are the legends still current at the Back of Beyond, but they are dwindling away. Even old Hogben could find it possible to say that "ghostesses" were already "quite out-o'-doors"—by which he meant that they were out of fashion. But he was bung-full of smuggling lore, and could illustrate his stories with object lessons, as he drove his steady course along the Stone Street. "'See dat tree," he would say, in passing a copse. "Dat's where de Ransleys"—naming a ferocious family of smugglers, men and women, notorious for their cruelties and outrages—"dat's where de Ransleys tied one of deir haases, before dey were taken off to Maidstone Gaol." The horse was starved to death, thus haltered, and the gang, who had been known to beat a Revenue officer to death, were almost heart-broken when they heard of it. Such contradictions are we all.

CHAPTER XIII

THE BACK OF BEYOND (*continued*)

If we continued along this straight road, the Mecca of the Stone Street carriers, Canterbury, would be reached again. Instead, we turn to the right, and in a mile and a half reach the Elham Valley and the hoary village of Lyminge, looking very new when viewed from a little distance, by reason of the sudden eruption of red-roofed villas come to disturb the ancient seclusion. Have a care how you pronounce the name of this village, lest by some uncovenanted rendering you proclaim yourself a stranger. The cautious in these matters always accost the first inhabitant met with, and ask him the name of the place, a method never known to fail unless the encounter takes place outside the post-office and the inhabitant be a crusty one who, curtly, and with an over-the-shoulder jerk of the thumb, says, "You'll find it written up there."

LYMINGE.

By the united testimony of the phonetic spelling of the thirteenth century and the twentieth century pronunciation of the natives, "Lyminge" should be enunciated with a short, not a long, "y" for the first syllable; while one should, for the second, pronounce as in "singe" or "hinge." Authority for the ancient pronunciation being the same as now is found in the name of a thirteenth-century rector, spelled "de Limminge," which clinches the matter. It is, however, quite other-guesswork with the meaning or the derivation of the name. One school of antiquaries finds its origin in the Latin name of the Stone Street, which when the Romans came was, they tell us, an ancient British trackway called the Heol-y-Maen, or Stone Path. The Romans reconstructed both the path and its name, which, in the Latinised "Via Limenea," was as near as they could get to the uncouth tongue of the Britons. Unfortunately for this ingenious theory, Lyminge is a mile and a half from the Stone Street. It really derived its name, in common with Lympne, from the Flumen Limenea, or river Limen, which once flowed down the valley, a considerable stream, now shrunken to a tiny brook.

LYMINGE CHURCH.

The Romans prevailed largely in these parts, and, despite friend Hogben, performed some wonderful things, even though "foreigners." They certainly colonised at Lyminge, in whose church walls the red Roman tiles from some shattered villa are plentifully worked in among the undoubted Saxon masonry. The present church is the successor of what is considered to have been the first Christian basilica erected under the Roman rule in this island, and reconstructed about A.D. 640 by Ethelburga, daughter of King Ethelbert, on the re-introduction of Christianity. Here that pious princess founded a Benedictine nunnery, and here, in the fulness of time, she died. Portions of her religious establishment long remained, and formed admirable pig-sties, but even those few relics have been improved away. Very much, however, remains in and around the church, to indicate its Roman origin and to prove the old theory that it was reared upon a building of three apsidal aisles. Indeed, the base of one of those same apses is laid open to view on the south side of the building, level with the gravel path. This south side of the church is eminently picturesque, with its wooden porch, and windows of widely-different ages and styles, together with the ancient flying buttress built against the south-east angle of the chancel.

The Elham Valley, in whose basin Lyminge lies nestled, runs up to Bridge and Canterbury, and a branch of the South-Eastern Railway runs down it, taking advantage of the easy gradients in a manner common to railways. Places in it are ceasing to be remote and can no longer strictly be said to be Beyond, much less at the Back of it. Thus we will not pursue this pleasant hollow in the hills very far, but will cut across to Acryse. But not before seeing Elham itself, the capital and metropolis of the vale.

OLD HOUSES AT ELHAM.

"E-lam"—for that, and not the more obvious way, is the correct local shibboleth—sits boldly in the lap of the hills, visible afar off. Those who hunt the fox with the East Kent Foxhounds know it well, for the kennels are situated here, but few else have made its acquaintance. It was once—in far-off times, when the ancient and beautiful houses in its one broad street were new —a market-town, and if it has lost its trade it has by no means relinquished its dignity. This is no place to speak at length of Elham church, whose tall tower and tapering spire command the valley, nor is it the place wherein to hold forth upon the library within the church, bequeathed some hundreds of years ago to the good folks of Elham by some old-world benefactor, strong in his belief in the civilising influence of literature when dispensed at the hands of the local clergyman—or perhaps merely anxious to be rid of a mass of useless rubbish. That library is reported to contain a valuable collection of Great Rebellion tracts; but what it does contain no Elhamite can with certainty tell you, because their reading runs in the lines of least resistance—which is equal to saying that they prefer the news columns of their weekly paper to the crabbed literature of that revolution which saved us from Popery more than two hundred years ago. For that reason alone the position of church librarian at Elham is a sinecure.

We have, for the purpose of seeing Elham, proceeded a little too far for

Acryse, and must retrace our steps, ascending the steep hillsides to the east for that purpose.

It is only by dint of much climbing that one reaches Acryse, for it tops the range of uplands that shut in the Elham valley. Climbing up the lane by which Master Marsh and his man Ralph descended, in the legend of "The Leech of Folkestone," the woods of Acryse are found clothing the crest and extending densely into a shrouded table-land, where the sun-rays percolate but dimly through a heavy overarching interlaced canopy of boughs. Acryse means "Oak Hill," but, whatever the character of these woods may once have been, the oak certainly is not the most numerous in them to-day. If one tree preponderates over any other species here, it is the beech, which in the dim light and closely-serried ranks has grown so spindly that it only begins to throw out branches at a height of some thirty or forty feet from the ground. The simpleton who could not see the wood for the trees is proverbial, but it is at first impossible to see Acryse, on account of the woods. And no wonder, for the woods are so large and Acryse so small. There is not even the semblance of a hamlet. The manor house and the adjoining manorial chapel form the whole of the place, except some scattered few cottages out of sight, for whose inhabitants the chapel serves the function of parish church. The Papillons, who once held the manor of Acryse, have long since relinquished it, and Mackinnons have for three generations past resided here. The butterfly crest of the old owners is therefore sought in vain in manor house or chapel. Chapel and house are discreetly secluded within the mossy woods, and only the diminutive spire of the one and some few glimpses of the outbuildings and bellcote of the other are gained between the clustering tree-stems. History, by association, is making at Acryse, for it is the seat of that Colonel Mackinnon who commanded the C.I.V. in the second Boer War.

ACRYSE.

If signs of human habitation are small here, those of bird-life are overwhelming. The woods of Acryse are one vast rookery. In winter, when the boughs are unclothed, their nests occupy every fork of the branches, and all the year they make their presence known, not only by the disfigurement of the stranger's clothing as he walks under their roosting-places, but by the rising and falling bursts of cawing that mark all hours of the day, like a perpetual session of Parliament with the Speaker absent and the Irish members in individual and collective possession of the House, each one talking "nineteen to the dozen," and each with a personal grievance to duly ventilate. For the note of the rookery is a distinctly querulous one, always in opposition. Occasionally, when the greater din dies down, grave and reverend —or, at least, deep and self-satisfied—individual voices are heard, like those of well-fed and paunchy ministers rising to defend their departments and themselves, with voices remonstrant, argumentative, or triumphant.

What the rooks find to talk about all day and every day might puzzle anyone who did not read the reports of Imperial Parliament; but those having once been read, there is no room for surprise.

It is only when evening approaches that the rookery is stilled, and even then only after a preliminary clamour from home-coming birds, in conclave, that makes one's ears sing again. After that deafening rally the voices are heard singly, bubbling and gobbling, until at last, when the rim of the sun sinks down below the horizon, the colony is at rest.

Leaving lonely Acryse amid a hoarse parting chorus from its rooks, we will turn our course towards Swingfield Minnis, and thence to St. John's, the scene of that lightest and brightest of the Legends, the "Witches' Frolic." We need expect to find no ruin, for Barham's description in the verse is altogether beside the mark. Thus he, in the character of Grandfather Ingoldsby, apostrophises it:

> I love thy tower, Grey Ruin,
> I joy thy form to see,
> Though reft of all, bell, cloister, and hall,
> Nothing is left save a tottering wall.

> Thou art dearer to me, thou Ruin Grey,
> Than the Squire's verandah, over the way;
>   And fairer, I ween, the ivy sheen
> That thy mouldering turret binds,
> Than the Alderman's house, about half a mile off,
> With the green Venetian blinds.

There is no alderman's house in the neighbourhood, with or without Venetian blinds, but that matters little.

It is by a succession of steeply rising and falling, winding and narrow country lanes that the Preceptory of the Knights Templars of St. John of Jerusalem, near Swingfield Minnis, is reached. Like so many other ancient religious establishments, it is now a farmstead. Not altogether picturesque, and wearing very few outward signs of antiquity, it might readily be passed by those not keenly in quest of it, except for the existence of the three tall Early English windows prominent in one of the gables. An inspection of the farmhouse proves that thrifty use has been made of the old buildings, the hall, the principal ancient feature, with fine old timber roof, being divided for domestic purposes into two floors. Modern walls and fireplaces combine to almost wholly alter the internal arrangements. A long, buttressed, monastic barn of great antiquity is pictured in Knight's *Old England*, published some sixty years ago, but it has long since disappeared in the insensate rage for "improvement," and there is very little of interest now to be seen outside the farmhouse. But whatever it lacks in picturesque aspect, the glamour of romance thrown over the spot by the legend redeems it from the commonplace.

THE PRECEPTORY, SWINGFIELD MINNIS.

Rival explanations of the singular name of Swingfield Minnis divide opinion as to whether the first word means "Swinefield" or "Sweyn's Field," but a striking confirmation of the theory that it is named after that Danish king, and of the vague records of his having achieved a victory here, was afforded by the discovery of a quantity of human bones in modern times, in the course of which were described by a newspaper as "some agricultural operations," when the ancient surrounding heath or common-land was, for the first time in its history, enclosed and broken into for cultivation. If we, in our commonplace way, translate "agricultural operations" into "ploughing," we shall probably be correct. The remains were at the time pronounced to be the relics of some long-forgotten fight. "Minnis" is a Cantise word for a piece of rough stony common, such as long existed here.

Barham, as freeholder in the district, was interested in this enclosure and was awarded his share of the spoil. "St. John's," the name by which the farm is known, is, as he says, in his note to the "Witches' Frolic," two miles from Tappington, but it certainly cannot be seen, as he would have us believe, over the intervening coppices, nor in any other way, as we presently discover on coming past Tappington into Denton, there joining on to a route described in an earlier chapter.

CHAPTER XIV

THE COASTWISE ROAD—FOLKESTONE TO DOVER AND SANDWICH

That is a toilsome road by which one leaves Folkestone for Dover. The chalk —"infinite" indeed, as Dickens said—the blinding glare of the sun upon it, the steep gradients, the rain-worn gullies, the tortuous curves, and the persistent up and up of Folkestone Hill, make the salt perspiration start from the wayfarer's brow and run smartly into his eyes. But when the hilltop is reached, where a once picturesque but now rebuilt inn, the "Valiant Sailor," stands, grand is the view backwards upon the town. That view is so sheer that the place looks all roof, and seems a squalid huddle-together of ill-arranged streets. No one, gazing down upon Folkestone from this view-point, would suspect the palatial and magnificent nature of its later growth.

It was but yester-year that the five miles length of cliff-top and chalky road on to Dover was solitary and marked by infrequent houses, but no longer do the crows and the seagulls hold undisturbed possession. It has never been a pleasant road, lying open and unfenced upon the roof of the cliffs and along an inhospitable country. Those whose way has lain along it have been grilled in summer and in winter pierced through and through by icy blasts that no hospitable hedgerows or kindly shelter of any description have served to lessen. Now these bleak and forbidding uplands are varied with brickfields, sporadic new houses, and blatant notice-boards offering building-land for sale, and they are not improved by the change. Greatly to be pitied is that cyclist who essays this road from the direction of Dover, for in that terrible continuous climb he affords the best comparison with the state of a good man struggling with undeserved adversity. "Surely," he thinks, "I shall soon come to the end of this rise"; but the white ribbon of the roadway rises ever before him, until, exhausted, he crests the hill at the "Valiant Sailor," where the staggering descent into Folkestone forbids him to ride down.

How different the case of the eastward-bound! No sooner is the climb from Folkestone completed than the long descent into Dover begins. Five miles away, down at the bottom of a cleft at the end of this chute, Dover Castle is blotted against the sky, and the cyclist has nothing to do but sit still and let the miles reel comfortably away, until the electric tramways at the outskirts of Dover are reached.

There is a point on this road between Folkestone and Dover that on moonlit nights makes a picture after Barham's own heart. When the full moon comes sailing up over the Castle Hill and floods the chalky road with light, leaving the town of Dover lost in the darkling valley of the Dour and the downs behind etched in a profound blackness upon the luminous heavens, then you recall those exquisite lines from the "Old Woman clothed in Grey":

> Oh! sweet and beautiful is Night, when the silver moon is
>   high,
> And countless stars, like clustering gems, hang sparkling in
>   the sky.

Yes; and night is more beautiful than day here, for the aching whiteness, the parching dryness, the arid bareness of the chalk highway and the folded hills are touched to romance by the cold majesty of the moon, whose light softens the austerities of the road, just as the dews assuage the lingering heats of day.

Tom Ingoldsby never, in the whole course of his writings, had much to say of Dover, and the legend of the "Old Woman clothed in Grey," tacked on to this ancient port, is really a Cambridgeshire story, hailing from Boxworth, near St. Ives. The incidents, he says, "happened a long time ago, I can't say exactly *how* long,"—which is rather vague:

> All that one knows is,
> It must have preceded the Wars of the Roses

Here he takes occasion to have another fling at Britton, in this footnote, where "Simpkinson of Bath" (whom we have already seen to be intended for that eminent antiquary) is made to confuse these historic campaigns with some family contentions: "An ancient and most pugnacious family," says our Bath friend. "One of their descendants, George Rose, Esq., late M.P. for Christchurch (an elderly gentleman now defunct), was equally celebrated for his vocal abilities and his wanton destruction of furniture when in a state of excitement. 'Sing, old Rose, and burn the bellows!' has grown into a proverb."

And so, indeed, for many centuries past it has, but no one has yet satisfactorily explained its origin. Many amusingly conflicting derivations of it have been given. One, as old as 1740, is found in the *British Apollo* of that year:

> In good King Stephen's days, the Ram,
> An ancient inn at Nottingham,
> Was kept, as our wise father knows,
> By a brisk female called Old Rose.
> Many like you, who hated thinking,
> Or any other theme but drinking,
> Met there, d'ye see, in sanguine hope,

To kiss their landlady and tope;
But one cross night, 'mongst many other,
The fire burnt not without great pother,
Till Rose, at last, began to sing,
And the cold blades to dance and spring;
So by their exercise and kisses
They grew as warm as were their wishes:
When, scorning fire, the jolly fellows,
Cried, "Sing, Old Rose, and burn the bellows."

An even earlier reference is found in Izaak Walton's *Angler*, where, in the second chapter, the Hunter proposes that they shall sing "Old Rose." Ingenuity has been let loose upon this subject, without much satisfaction obtained. "Let's singe Old Rose and burn libellos," is a wild variant, given as the cries of schoolboys on the eve of holidays, and signifying, "Let's singe Old Rose's wig and burn our books"; but we are not enlightened as to that school of which this "Old Rose" was principal. This "explanation" is, in fact, so much sage stuffing for green goslings, and we will not be so simple as to partake of it.

Ingoldsby advises the visitor to Dover to dine at the "York" or the "Ship," and then to set out for the Maison Dieu and there ask for the haunted house, the scene of the Old Woman's post-mortem visitations. Where are the "York" or the "Ship" to-day? You would as vainly seek them as the haunted house; but they did, at the time he wrote, actually exist, which the house never did. The Maison Dieu, however, was, and is, very real, but is more intelligibly sought, to the Dover townsfolk's ears, under the title of the town hall.

As for the Priory, whence the mercenary Father Basil of the legend came, that vanished long ago in disestablishment and ruin, only a few portions, including the ancient gatehouse, being included in the modern buildings of Dover College. The "Priory" station of the Chatham and Dover line takes its name from this ancient religious house. Some records of the Prior and his Benedictine monks who were housed here still remain. It would seem that they were, at the last, when the Priory was dissolved, a very bad lot indeed, and quite merited disestablishment, if nothing more. They preferred amorous intrigues to mortifying the flesh with the scourgings, cold water, and stale crusts represented by the orthodox as the staple fare and daily discipline of such. They were veritable Friar Tucks, these jolly monks of Dover, so far as provand was concerned, while their morals left much to be desired, as may be judged when we read the testimony of the Royal commissioners who were sent hither to report upon their conduct. Those emissaries gave no notice of their advent; in fact, the first intimation the Prior had of their quite unceremonious visit was when the noise of their bursting open the door of his bedroom (not, if you please, his "cell") woke both him and the lady who shared his bed. The commissioners turned her out, in that lay brother's costume in which she had gained admittance to the monastery. Such historical evidence refutes the charges of flippant injustice towards the olden Roman Catholic times of which Ingoldsby has often been accused.

THE "LONE TREE."

In quest of the "Marston Hall" of "The Leech of Folkestone," and of traces of Master Marsh we must leave Dover, and, climbing the steep and winding Castle Hill, come, under the frowning keep and warder towers of that great fortress, to the high, bare, chalky table-land that stretches from this point to Deal and Sandwich. It is an open, unfenced road at the beginning, and so shadeless that a very striking elm solitary by the wayside is known far and wide as the "Lone Tree." This isolated object has a story, told with a thorough belief in its truth. It seems that, a great many years ago, a soldier of the Castle garrison murdered a comrade on this spot by felling him with a stick he carried. No one saw the deed done, and he was so convinced that the crime would never be traced that he thrust the elm-stick in the ground, declaring that he was safe so long as it did not take root.

His regiment was shortly afterwards ordered abroad, and it was not until many years had passed that he was again at Dover. Once there, a morbid curiosity took him to the scene of his crime, where, horror-stricken, he found that stick a flourishing tree. He confessed, and was duly executed.

It is a legend exactly after Ingoldsby's own heart, but perhaps he never heard of it, for it does not appear in his writings.

From this point, two miles distant from Dover, the way goes straight; East Langdon, for which we are making, lying in the hug of the downs, a mile away to the left, lost to view between those swelling contours and in midst of clustered trees.

It was to this parish that "Thomas Marsh of Marston," the hero of that prose legend, "The Leech of Folkestone," really belonged. He resided at Martin, Marten, or Marton Hall, in the neighbouring hamlet of Martin, whose name is thus variously and impartially spelled by post-office, finger-posts, county historians and other authorities, who to this day have not been able to decide which is the true and proper rendering. East Langdon, on closer acquaintance, resolves itself into a remote, huddled-up village of very small dimensions, situated on a narrow lane that does duty for a road, and consisting of a parish church, an inn, two or three farms, a rectory, and some agricultural labourers' cottages—the whole knowing little of the outside world, and apparently content with that knowledge. It centres around the church and Church Farm, pictured here, and by that sketch, much more eloquently than by any mass of verbiage, shall you see how grim and hard-featured a place it is. The church has latterly been restored, and the monument in its chancel to the veritable Thomas Marsh of the legend again made whole. It had fallen, about 1850, from its place on the north wall of the chancel, and was broken in many pieces, the fragments being preserved in a cupboard in the vestry. Under such circumstances, and fully cognisant of the atrocious things that have elsewhere been wrought, all over the country, in the name of "restoration," it is with a shock of surprise that the pilgrim finds it at all. But here it is, a black marble tablet surrounded by an ornamental framing of white stone or marble, and bearing a long Latin inscription to "Thomas Marsh, of Marton." He is stated to have been born in 1583, and to have died in 1634.

EAST LANGDON.

132

"MARSTON HALL."

The hamlet of Martin, three-quarters of a mile distant, is, possibly from its proximity to the railway station of Martin Mill, larger at this day than the parent village. Why the Chatham and Dover Railway authorities should choose to christen the station after the great wooden windmill that towers up, black and striking, beside the line, instead of simply by the name of the place, is not evident, for there is no other "Martin" on the railway from which it might otherwise be desirable to distinguish this. The hamlet itself overlooks the railway, from its superior ridge. You come steeply uphill into it, through an overarching bower of hedgerow greenery enclosing a hollow road, strikingly like a Devonshire lane, and the more remarkable and pleasing because set in midst of downs so generally treeless. Prominent in the street of Martin is the great farmhouse known as "Martin House," that "Marston Hall" of the story of Master Marsh's bewitchment, and once the manor house. Portions of it may be as old as the early seventeenth century, but it has been remodelled in a particularly hideous manner, and the side of it towards the farmyard smeared over with "compo," or similar abomination.

THE "THREE HORSESHOES," GREAT MONGEHAM.

Regaining the high-road at Ringwould, Walmer is passed and Upper Deal, with the sea and the crowded shipping of the Downs and the white cliffs of France forming a striking picture on the right. It is worth while turning off, a quarter of a mile to the left, to see the little village called, magnificently, Great Mongeham, just beyond Deal, for its quaint "Three Horseshoes" inn still displays a curious wrought-iron sign originally made in 1735, a very striking object, overhanging the road.

The high bleak downs gradually sink down as Sandwich is neared, and give place to flats. Away on the right, mile upon mile of blown sand and dunes, tussocky with coarse grass, border the sea, and inland stretch the vast unfenced fields of corn, beans, or oats that are so characteristic of this corner of Kent, and of the Isle of Thanet.

Sandwich is always described as a "dead port," but we have already seen that New Romney is more dead—if so Irish an expression may be allowed. By a flat, straight stretch of road that ancient member of the Cinque Ports is reached, past a row of tall poplars, the ancient Hospital of St. Bartholomew and—the railway station, which is absurdly brisk for a place supposed to have died and been buried about three hundred years ago. Past this unmistakable evidence of post-mortem activity, are the town walls, now, in passing, seen to be grassy ramparts, tree-shaded, with walks, and below them little dykes and runnels—a very beautiful scene which tells us that Sandwich has so far retired from business that it does not actually grow; although, as for being dead, why, there, at the other extremity of the town, where the navigable channel of the Stour flows and conveys those ships up and down that still trade here, you may see loading and unloading still going forward, and port-dues being collected and all manner of bustle.

But Sandwich is a very staid and grave old town. It knows—its ancient harbour being long centuries ago silted up—that it cannot compete with modern ports, and so folds its hands and accepts the minor part now assigned to it, and lives in the ancient ways; which is why we love "Sannidge"—to speak in the fashion of those who live there.

But it really was once a great port and its past lives in history. Many were its dramatic moments. Such an one was that when Becket, the banished Archbishop of Canterbury, returning after years of exile, landed from a boat in the haven. He had a premonition of his violent ending, for he embarked upon his return with the significant words, *"Vado in Angliam mori,"* "I go into England to die." The people knew of his coming, and a cross erected in the bows of the boat that put him ashore made the identity of its occupants certain a great way off. He was popular with the masses, who crowded around him at the landing-stage, eager for a blessing from the "father of the orphans and protector of the widows." Thence he set forward, without delay, for Canterbury, by way of Ash.

Let us pluck another incident at hazard from the long roll of years. It is toward the close of 1415, and days grow chill and nights bitter. The war with France has ended with every circumstance of glory for England. Nine thousand Frenchmen lie dead at Agincourt, proving on their bodies the truth of the English arrow-flight and the prowess of the English men-at-arms. Harry V. has been received on his home-coming at Dover with the rapturous applause of an elated nation, and London has sealed that welcome. By detachments, the rank and file of the expedition slowly return home—some landing at Southampton, some at Dover, others here; each man laden with some article of loot; all wearied, hungry, and out of humour, because when they marched to our stronghold of Calais they were refused shelter and sustenance, the garrison of that town being afraid of running short of provisions.

They look, doubtless, for an enthusiastic welcome on their home-coming; banners waving, hand-shaking, tumultuous cheers. What do they find? Why, this: that the edge has been taken off the fame of their exploits by those who returned first, and that the townsfolk of Sandwich are cold—cold as the November wind, and their reception as forbidding as the lowering sky. Even so did Jacob obtain the blessing of Isaac, and Esau was deprived of his birthright. No blessing, no feasting, no drinking for them, save for money down, and money they have none; so that they are fain to sell their booty as best they may, to buy bread and lodging. Callous Sandwich? Nay, but history has repeated itself quite recently on the same lines; glory is as brilliant a thing as a soap-bubble, and as evanescent.

135

But one must be done with these mosaics from history. The town reached a great prosperity when Edward III. in 1377 removed the staple here, from Queenborough; but that was its high-water mark. The ebb did not at once begin, for still, in 1470, the annual customs revenue of the port amounted to £17,000 and ninety-five ships were registered as belonging to the place. There were then 1,500 sailors in the town.

But in the time of Henry VIII. the sand, long threatening, had closed the harbour to ships of any considerable burthen, and decay set in. The port declined, but, owing to the large settlement of Hollander and Huguenot weavers in Sandwich, the place did not shrink to nothing, and perhaps it is due to them that it exists at all.

ST. PETER'S, SANDWICH.

From the tall, Dutch-like tower of St. Peter's the curfew-bell is nightly tolled, as for seven hundred years the custom has been. The sexton's annual stipend for performing this nightly service is £8; not a great sum for a corporate town to yearly disburse, but something of a consideration for a place like Sandwich, whose commercial greatness is now only a thing of history and ancient repute. Thus it was that in 1833 the unbroken continuity of the curfew from Norman times was seriously threatened, in a proposal of the Corporation to discontinue the practice, and the payment for it. Sentimental considerations, however, prevailed, and thus it is that the nightly bell continues to ring over the melancholy sand-flats, as of yore. But economical considerations again, in quite recent years, threatened the old custom on the same grounds, when, about 1895, it was proposed to discontinue the ringing and to save the money for more practical purposes. Again, however, sentiment prevailed, and what the old inhabitants call "the old charter" continues.

This church of St. Peter, one of the three possessed by the town, is its most notable landmark, and from all points of view stamps the town with a distinct alien appearance. It is by no means the principal church—that honour belongs to St. Clement's, whose massive and highly decorated Norman tower is second only to that of New Romney. But St. Clement's tower is only of medium height; that of St. Peter is tall and stark, and is, moreover, capped with an extraordinary turret of distinctly Dutch feeling. Sometimes you laugh at it and think it something bulbous and onion-like; at other times, and from some points of view, it is impressive, rather than absurd. If it were away, Sandwich would lose much of its individuality. It is not an old tower, as ages in churches go, and was built only in the years immediately following 1661, when the older tower fell, and not only involved itself in complete ruin, but demolished the whole length of the south aisle, and, with the bells, buried the whole interior of the church three feet deep in what a contemporary account calls "rubidge." When the inhabitants set to work to repair the damage, they did not restore the destroyed aisle, but just walled up the arches and inserted the quaint Dutch-like windows still remaining. The tower they rebuilt with bricks economically manufactured out of the harbour mud, which, judging from the number of houses built of the same material, seems to have been as plentiful a deposit then as now. The Hollander character of the tower and of the town in general owed its being to the existence at that time of a very large Flemish and Walloon colony, originally formed in Queen Elizabeth's reign, when the persecuted weavers and others from the Low Countries came here as refugees and were welcomed as settlers, not only in Kent, but in many other districts of England. The Sandwich colony numbered some four hundred at the beginning, but they gradually became absorbed in intermarriages, until, as a separate race, they ceased to exist. But in that period, while they retained their national manners and architectural style, these "gentile and profitable strangers" did, as we see, succeed in impressing the place with their personality to a remarkable degree.

Thus, then, St. Peter's tower dominates the view far and near. St. Mary's tower fell six years later, but was not rebuilt, save in a stumpy and inconspicuous way. St. Clement's tower suffered restoration in 1886; the churchwardens obtained the necessary funds by the expedient of selling the bells!

CHAPTER XV

SANDWICH TO THE VILLE OF SARRE

Sandwich ends at the Barbican, the foreign-looking watergate that spans the road on the hither side of the Stour. Down to the left, away from the road to Pegwell Bay and Ramsgate, can be seen from this point the dark ruin of Richborough, and directly on that road, to the right, a belt of sparse woodland, a clump of thin, wiry trees, insufficiently nourished on the sandy and pebbly soil. In midst of this, solitary and surrounded with an atmosphere of melancholy, is an absolutely uninteresting modern house. These trees and this house form all that remains of the once important and flourishing port of Stonar, or Lundenwic, an early rival of Sandwich itself. The spot and an adjoining one are now marked on the maps as "Great and Little Stonar." The history of that vanished town is vague and fragmentary, but enthralling, like some half-told tale of faëry. Its very incertitude renders it into the likeness of a city of dream, the product of a magician's wand, blighted by uncanny spell. What, then, do we know of Stonar? Just this: that in the long ago, in A.D. 456, the Britons under Vortimer, after being deserted by the Roman legions, secured one of their few victories over the invading pagan Saxons on this spot, a spot fixed by the Latin annalist in the phrase, *"In campo juxta Lapidem Tituli."* It was near here, therefore, in these flats, that the battle was fought, and the place seems to derive its name of Stonar from that same Latin *"Lapidem."* Now it is remarkable that the Kentish coast is rich in place-names including the word "stone." Littlestone near Old Romney, is an example—Folkestone another, and the most prominent—the ancient *"Lapis Populi"* of Latin records. But from what stones those original names proceeded who shall say?

THE BARBICAN, SANDWICH.

The British victory was but an interlude in an almost unbroken series of defeats inflicted upon that unhappy people by the ruthless Saxons, who presently bore down all opposition on the Kentish shores, and established themselves here. It was they who founded the original town of Stonar, on a sandspit even then forming at the mouth of the River Stour and the entrance to the channel of the Wantsume, dividing the Isle of Thanet from the mainland of Kent; and the Roman fortress of Rutupium, the vast shell of ruined Richborough that we see to-day, overlooking the surrounding marshes from its rising vantage-ground, was converted by them into a fortress-palace for their kings.

SANDWICH, FROM GREAT STONAR.

When, in the course of time, the Saxons had possessed themselves of the country and had at last become luxurious and less warlike, they were in turn attacked by the fiercer Danes. Prominent among the many bloody fights waged for the mastery was the second battle of Stonar, fought here between the forces of Torkill the Dane and the Saxon king, Edmund Ironside, in 1009. It was one of those exceptional victories for the Saxons that now and again cheered them in their long series of disasters.

Stonar's alternative name of Lundenwic seems to have derived from the extensive trade with London, but of the vanished town and its records we know next to nothing. Only this, indeed, that its rivalry with Sandwich was fierce, and that Sandwich was gaining the advantage and Stonar decaying when the ill-fated town was entirely destroyed and swept away by the sea in the great storm of 1365, when Sandwich not only took all its trade, but assumed its alias of "Lundenwic" as well. "It is an ill wind that blows no one any good," says the old saw, and this was worth much to Sandwich. If tempests—or "tompuses," as the Kentish folk, in their quaint speech, call them—were of such destructive powers to-day, insurance would cease to be the lucrative business it now is.

Richborough, that frowns so grim down upon the Stour meadows and the flat Sandwich and Ramsgate road, is a favourite haunt of archæologists. It rises, rugged walls and bulging bastions, from low, earthy cliffs, ivy-clad in places, and shrouded by dense thickets of brushwood, where the earth falls away to the levels. The secretive ivy, incredibly aged, clasps the hoary masonry with a tenacity that will not allow of severance. They will live and die together, those walls and that "rare old plant, the ivy green."

The view from Richborough is comprehensive and varied. Away to the right is Sandwich, a mass of clustered roofs and spars and rigging, dominated, of course, by that Dutch-like cupola of St. Peter's, resembling some gigantic onion of fairy-lore; and away again to the left goes the curving shore, to Pegwell Bay and Ramsgate, with the white cliffs standing out to sea, as bolt upright as though they had been sliced out. The houses and some of the more prominent public buildings of Ramsgate peer over the edge of the down.

The railway that, taking advantage of the levels, runs between Sandwich and Ramsgate under these walls of the aged Roman castle is not an unromantic feature. Its living commercialism serves to contrast eloquently the methods of to-day and those of an Empire dead these fifteen hundred years. He must be a soulless signalman who does not, in his cabin placed under the shadow of that wall, sometimes let his imagination loose and, conjuring up the past, people those ramparts again with the helmeted sentries of old Rome.

More than 140,000 coins, Roman and Saxon, are said to have been, at one time and another, picked up within and around Richborough. That is why the visitor to Sandwich hastens at the earliest opportunity along those two miles that separate the ruins from the town, and is explanatory of his exploring zeal in turning over the clods with his foot and probing the light earth with his walking-stick. Alack! the statement that so great a number of coins have been found means perhaps that the last are gone, rather than that a hundred thousand or so remain. If the ploughman still finds anything, he keeps the fact to himself; but certainly, if any personal efforts of the present historian may count for testimony, there is a plentiful lack of anything but heavy clay in these fields. No precious fibula, no golden coin, nay, not even a humble copper *denarius* rewarded his anxious efforts, and the ware of Samos was equally to seek.

RICHBOROUGH, AND THE KENTISH COASTLINE TOWARDS RAMSGATE.

Here we are well within the Isle of Thanet, whose name, as generally is the case, is of uncertain origin. "Thanatos," the "Isle of Death," suggested some commentator in the bygone years, but he did not bolster up his derivation by telling us in what way it was so deadly. Perhaps in the wrecks of its coast. In other respects, Thanet is the Isle of Good Health, of rude, hungry, boisterous health; and in summer the Isle of Cockneys. Does it not contain Ramsgate —"rollicking Ramsgate",—and Margate the merry, whose name—I am sorry —always reminds me of margarine? It was at Margate, upon Jarvis's Jetty, that "Mr. Simpkinson" met the "little vulgar boy" who did him so very brown, but I am not going to Margate to see the Jetty; which has been greatly altered since Jarvis caused it to rise out of the vasty deep. Margate is mentioned only that once in the *Ingoldsby Legends* and Ramsgate not at all, and so I shall cut them out of my journey, and make across inland, over the high ridge at Acol, to Reculver.

The road is flat, the surface good, and from Sandwich to Ebbsfleet is an enjoyable run. At Ebbsfleet there has been lately erected a tall granite cross to mark where St. Augustine landed and reintroduced Christianity in A.D. 597. Perhaps not everyone knows that he was sent against his will on this mission by the Pope, and that it was only grumbling he came. Not altogether so saintly as we might, not inquiring closely, suppose—a morose and masterful man.

Through Minster lies our way—Minster-in-Thanet—reached by lanes of the charmingest, with overarching trees; very beautiful, and filled in summer with other things not so lovely: with such eye-sorrows and ear-torments as dusty

141

brake-parties clamant with the latest comic songs and energetically performing upon cornets and concertinas; little vulgar boys, descendants, possibly, of Mr. Simpkinson's young friend, turning cart-wheels in the dust for casual pence. The brake-proprietors of Margate and Ramsgate, conscious that such tree-shaded spots are rare in Thanet, have taken these under their protection, and advertise "Twelve miles drives through the pretty lanes, 1/-." Minster is therefore a paradise of beanfeasters and the inferno of pilgrims, literary or other.

THE SMUGGLER'S LEAP.

To find the "Smuggler's Leap" one must make as for Acol. "Near this hamlet of Acol," says Ingoldsby, in a fictitious quotation prefixed to the fine legend of Smuggler Bill and Exciseman Gill and their doings, "is a long-disused chalk-pit of formidable depth, known by the name of the 'Smuggler's Leap.' The tradition of the parish runs that a riding-officer from Sandwich, called Anthony Gill, lost his life here in the early part of the eighteenth century, while in pursuit of a smuggler. The smuggler's horse *only*, it is said, was found crushed beneath its rider. The spot has, of course, been haunted ever since." For the original of this quotation, the reader is referred to a "Supplement to Lewis's History of Thanet, by the Reverend Samuel Pegg, A.M., Vicar of Gomersham," supposed to have been published by a "W. Bristow, Canterbury, 1796"; but Ingoldsby, who composed the legend, invented his quotation as well, and those who seek the Reverend Samuel Pegg's "Supplement" will not find it.

But if so much be imaginative, the smuggling exploits common in the district a hundred and thirty years ago, as recorded in the Kentish newspapers, were in many respects like that celebrated in the Ingoldsby legend. The *Kentish Gazette* of Saturday, November 22nd, 1777, gives a case in point: "On

Monday last Mr. Harris, Officer of Excise, and Mr. Wesbeach, Surveyor of the Customs at Ramsgate, attended by six dragoons, met with a body of smugglers at Birchington, consisting of at least a hundred and fifty, armed with loaded whips and bludgeons. After a sharp skirmish, in which the smugglers had many of their horses shot, they made a very regular retreat, losing 8 gallons of brandy, 96 gallons of Geneva, 162 lb. of Hyson tea, and five horses."

MONKTON.

The chalk-pit, too, is sufficiently real. Crossing the open fields, spread starkly to the sky, between Monkton and Cleve Court, it is found on the Ramsgate road, opposite the "Prospect" inn, where it still gapes as deep and wide as ever. Do not, however, if you wish to be impressed with the truth of Ingoldsby's romantic description, view it by the brilliant sunlight of a summer's day, because at such times the great cleft in the dull white of the chalk does not properly proclaim its immensity. It is only when the evening shadows fall obliquely into the old chalk-pit that you applaud the spirit of those lines:

It's enough to make one's flesh to creep
To stand on that fearful verge, and peep
Down the rugged sides so dreadfully steep,
Where the chalk-pit yawns full sixty feet deep.

When Ingoldsby wrote there were, according to his testimony, "fifty intelligent fly-drivers" plying upon Margate pier, who would convey the curious to the spot for a guerdon which they term "three bob." Cycles and electric tramways have nowadays so sorely cut up the trade of the intelligent that few of those depressed individuals remain.

MONKTON.

Coming into Monkton, a scattered village on the way to Sarre, the church, directly facing the road, makes, with the old stocks on a grassy bank, a pretty picture. The indications of arches, seen in the sketch, show that there was once a north aisle to this church. The parish owes its name to the fact that the manor was anciently the property of Christ Church Monastery, Canterbury.

The whole of this district is covered by the legend of the "Smuggler's Leap." The "smuggling crew" dispersed in all directions before the customs-house officers.

> Some gallop this way, and some gallop that,
> Through Fordwich Level, o'er Sandwich Flat ...
> Those in a hurry Make for Sturry,
> With Customs House officers close in their rear,
> Down Rushbourne Lane, and so by Westbere.
>   None of them stopping But shooting and popping,
> And many a Customs House bullet goes slap
> Through many a three-gallon tub like a tap,
>   And the gin spurts out, And squirts all about;
> And many a heart grew sad that day,
> That so much good liquor was so thrown away.

> Down Chislett Lane, so free and so fleet,
>   Rides Smuggler Bill, and away to Up Street;
> Sarre Bridge is won—Bill thinks it fun,
> Ho! ho! the old tub-gauging son of a gun.

We, too, will ride into Sarre.

Sarre was, and is still technically, a ville of the port of Sandwich, governed by a Deputy whose functions are now merely decorative. He still, however, as of old, swears fealty to King and port. These historical facts explain those notices, "Town of Sarre" and "Ville de Sarre" prominently displayed on the houses at the Canterbury and Thanet ends of the village respectively.

The bridge gained by Smuggler Bill is that which joins Kent and the Isle of Thanet, the successor of that original pont built in 1485, on the site of "the common ferry when Thanet was full iled." It is not a romantic bridge nowadays, and has its many thousands of counterparts. Beneath its commonplace arch the sluggish waters of a branch of the Stour go wandering away, right and left, along the old narrowed channel of the once broad and navigable Wantsume, where the sea once flowed, and the Roman galleys and triremes, the Saxon and Danish prows, and the Norman and early English ships, came and went; and only a shallow stream, no wider than a horse could jump, choked with reeds and snags, divides the former "Isle" and the mainland.

Sarre is picturesque in parts, and in other parts quite distressingly ugly. It is, indeed, a peculiarity of Kent, overrun from the earliest times by Cockneys, that many of its buildings touch the deepest depth of ugliness, vulgarity, and unsuitability. The Cockney has come forth of his Cockaigne, and builded, after his sort, great grey-brick houses in the model of the houses in towns, where of necessity, being in streets and shouldered by neighbours, they run to height and unrelieved squareness. Sarre contains exactly such an example, in one of the two inns—one never can recollect the name of a commonplace inn —that minister not only to the wants of Sarre, but were halting-places for the Margate and Ramsgate coaches in the old days, just as they are "pull-ups" for the brake-parties of the present time.

THE "VILLE OF SARRE."

The artist can dodge the hideous inn out of his sketch and can make a pretty view of Sarre, but unless he adopts the tactics of a Turner, and takes a piece here and another there, and so fits them together in a composition of his own, he cannot get into one view the quaint old barn-yards, with their curious barns standing, for fear of the rats, shouldered off the ground on stone staddles; nor can he include the bridge, the stream, and the long, poplar-lined road into the village. In no case could he bring in the time-worn tower of a village church, that sanctifies a sketch, for Sarre is godless and graceless and owns no church, its inhabitants finding their nearest place of worship at St. Nicholas-at-Wade, nearly two miles distant.

CHAPTER XVI

SARRE AND RECULVER TO CANTERBURY

The rows of feathery poplars lining the causeway road out of Sarre towards Canterbury give it, for a little distance, the look of a French road. But they presently cease, and it becomes for some miles a singularly dreary way. All the more excuse, therefore, for adventuring away from it across country to Reculver, celebrated by Ingoldsby in the "Brothers of Birchington."

Chislett village, through which the route lies, shows prominently from its ridge—or, rather, its church does. A church it is of singular outline, viewed from a distance, and calculated to entice the inquisitive away from the direct road, only to find that the bizarre appearance is caused by the spire having been almost wholly shorn off at some time not specified, and the stump suffered to remain. For the rest, Chislett is sufficiently interesting in the wheat and swede and mangold way, but not otherwise attractive, unless the stocks, still preserved in the churchyard, may be mentioned.

The route from here to Reculver is a five miles long stretch of scrubwoods, through the hamlet of Marsh Row. These rabbity solitudes lead at last to the low, broken, earthy coast presenting a weak and dissolving barrier to an encroaching sea between Herne Bay and Birchington. Midway between those two watering-places stands the gaunt ruin of that ancient church built within the Roman castle of Regulbium, to which its name in mutilated form has descended. Its skeleton towers rise over the hillside, minatory, as we descend toward the sea.

CHISLETT.

Reculver is popularly—and mistakenly—spoken and written of in the plural, "Reculvers." There is no real warranty, in the derivation of the name, for what our grandfathers would have called a "vulgar error." We can clearly trace the place-name from the Roman times, when it was "Regulbium," to the days of the Saxon King, Ethelbert, when it had been changed into "Raculf Ceastre," and thence, by way of half a hundred grotesque spellings in ancient historical documents, to the form it now bears. Never, save by modern writers of guide-books, has it been spoken of in the plural, and the only possible reason for their doing so must be a real ignorance of its history and a belief that the twin towers of the ruined church are themselves the "Reculvers." This is no attempt to right the wrong: that would be a hopeless task, and a thankless. A mistake set afoot so long ago and so popular is not to be discredited, and "Reculvers" this will remain, certainly so long as there are *two* towers.

In Roman times the fortress of Regulbium stood at some little distance from the sea, on the only available firm ground, a gentle rounded hill rising from the surrounding marshes. Now that the sea has for centuries been advancing upon the spot, this hill has been half washed away, and its remaining section shows as a low cliff, with the gaunt towers of the mediæval church rising from it. This church is the successor of that built within the walls of the Roman castle in Saxon times, as a monument of the downfall of Paganism and the triumph of Christianity.

So long ago as 1780 the sea had begun to threaten it, and the great north wall of the castle fell one night into the advancing tide, leaving the monument to Christianity in a very exposed condition, while the bones of the forgotten inhabitants were washed away out of the churchyard, just as those of Warden, in Sheppey, are at this day. Instead of making any attempt to save the church, the authorities began in 1809 to demolish it, only halting when they reached the twin towers. The surrounding farmers found the building-stones very useful for pig-sties and cow-sheds, and cared not a rap whether they were Norman or Early English. There were, indeed, some Roman columns in the church. They had come from the pagan basilica within the castle, but that did not hinder their being cast aside with the rest. In 1860 one was discovered, one of its stones doing duty as a garden-roller. It was, with another column, rescued from further desecration, and the two have been set up in the Cathedral Close at Canterbury.

RECULVER.

The vicarage was also abandoned in 1809, but not pulled down. It was converted into a public-house, which long stood here under the sign of the "Hoy." The existing inn is the "King Ethelbert."

The twin towers of Reculver church form a portion of the former west front. They are of Norman and Early English date, and, constructed as they were largely of the materials of the ruined Roman buildings, are rich in fragments of tile. The towers were erected to serve as a sea-mark, to warn vessels beating up for the Swale and the Medway of the dangerous Columbine Sand, and their origin has from time immemorial been the subject of the legend of the "Twin Sisters," which tells how the Abbess of the Benedictine Priory of Davington and her sister, voyaging to fulfil a vow made to Our Lady of Broadstairs, were wrecked here for lack of a sea-mark. The Abbess was saved, but her sister was drowned, and, as a combined thank-offering for her own escape and by way of memorial to her sister, that holy woman erected the twin towers, to serve all mariners sailing by. Barham perverted the legend in his "Brothers of Birchington." Perhaps the temptation to alliteration was too strong to be resisted, and then the idea came to him of rejecting the familiar story and using in its stead an old monastic tale of how there were two brothers, the one pious and the other given up to all manner of evil courses, and how the Devil came for the wrong one by mistake and was obliged to restore him. In the Ingoldsby legend the brothers become Robert and Richard de Birchington, and their vow it was, he tells us, which produced the famous sea-mark:

Well—there the "Twins" stand
On the verge of the land,
To warn mariners off from the Columbine Sand,
And many a poor man have Robert and Dick
By their vow caused to 'scape, like themselves, from Old
Nick.

The mariners of old never failed as they passed to bare their heads and pray to Our Lady or Reculver. It is said that a good omen was argued by them if the towers were clearly seen in passing, and evil if they were hidden by fog; but, when we consider the dangers of the sea in fogs, there seems less superstition in those ideas than sheer common-sense.

The towers have for many years been maintained by the Trinity House, according to the tablet over the doorway: "These towers, the remains of the once venerable Church of Reculver, were purchased of the Parish by the Corporation of the Trinity House of Deptford Strond in the year 1810, and groynes laid down at their expense to protect the cliff on which the church had stood. When the ancient spires were afterwards blown down, the present substitutes were erected, to render the towers still sufficiently conspicuous to be useful to navigation.—Captain Joseph Cotton, Deputy Master, in the year 1819."

Returning to Chislett and the breathless route of Smuggler Bill and his companions, Up Street hamlet, and Westbere are passed; Westbere itself in a deep hollow on a slip road plunging down romantically from that dreary highway. Then comes the long, bricky, dusty, gritty village of Sturry, whose name is taken from the River Stour, on which it stands, or rather, in which it stood, for it was once encircled by that now shrunken stream, and its original style was "Esturei," or "Stour Island." In midst of the village a turning to the left will lead the explorer to a little jewel of a place, lying forgotten by the Stour banks. He leaves populous Sturry behind, and comes, over little brick bridges as hump-backed as Quilp or Quasimodo, and by rustling alders, into a spot long since retired from worldly activities—enters, in fact, that decayed port of Canterbury, Fordwich.

FORDWICH.

Canterbury was once a seaport! How incredible it seems, now that Whitstable, the nearest point on the coast, is seven miles away, and the Stour so small a stream that even for rowing-boats it is at the present time scarce navigable. Yet to this very village of "Fordige" as the local speech has it, the salt tide came up the estuary in days well within the historic period. Not merely vague Romans, but historical personages—palpable human beings who have personally left great flat-footed, heavy-handed marks on the pages of our national story—have landed at the still-existing quay, at which it is even yet possible for one to land from a skiff, and so to parallel experiences for one brief glorious moment of historic self-consciousness with no less a personage than the Black Prince himself, who stepped ashore here from no skiff, but directly from the caravel that brought him across the Channel, fresh from his cruelties in Guienne and Spain. Those who welcomed him home—the Mayor and burgesses of Fordwich—were as cruel and savage as he in their unchivalric municipal way; the times were sodden with cruelty, supersaturated with ferocity, and the rejoicings at the warrior's home-coming did but serve as an afternoon's respite for those petty malefactors who awaited their doom in the two dark and dismal cells even yet existing beneath the old town hall and court house standing so picturesquely by this self-same quay. Not the whole of that curious building can claim so great an age, for the general aspect of it is scarce earlier than Elizabethan times. Indeed, it has latterly been made to look quite smart and neat, its nodding roof carefully squared, the lichen and stonecrop removed, and some nice new brickwork here and there inserted. "Restoration" seeks out the veriest holes and corners and culs-de-sac of the land, and "makes up" old buildings into new, like old dowagers masquerading as girls again.

Fordwich town hall filled many functions. In it were transacted all the business affairs of the old port; in it, too, justice was dealt out in rough and ready fashion to the miscreants of yore, and executed swiftly, and still more roughly and readily, outside. The justice of the Cinque Ports, of which Fordwich was a member, was by no means tempered with mercy, and was as blood-thirsty as those early laws of the Israelites duly set forth with much horrifying circumstantiality in Leviticus. Theves Lane, in Fordwich, led in ancient times to "Thefeswelle," the well in which convicted thieves were judicially drowned. Thieves with a preference for the easiest death commonly selected Dover for their operations in those times, for when the inevitable happened, the Dover authorities flung them from the cliff-top, and so they ended swiftly and mercifully with broken necks, a better way than being dropped down a well and the lid then put on, as here at Fordwich, or being buried alive or smothered in the harbour mud, after the Sandwichstyle.

FORDWICH TOWN HALL.

The dungeons beneath the town hall are provided with only a narrow barred opening, shuttered from the outside and admitting the least possible rays of light. On their walls may yet be seen the many scrawls of old-time prisoners. In one cell were secured those who had offended against the municipal authority of Fordwich, and in the other the captives of the Monastery of St. Augustine in Canterbury were laid by the heels; for two jurisdictions, the cause of many jealousies, ruled here. In none was there more heat shown than in the sole right and privilege of fishing for trout at Fordwich, claimed by the monastery and bitterly disputed by the port.

The rough, whitewashed interior of the court-room is simple but highly curious. The primitive bench and bar where prisoners were arraigned and causes heard are still here. Prosecutors had a difficult task in those days. Sometimes the court would decide that ordeal by battle was the best way of settling a dispute—a mean way, it will be acknowledged, of shirking its judicial responsibilities—and would secure seats outside to witness the fray, which suggests too engrossing a love of sport; at other times, when the court did patiently hear and adjudicate upon plaints, it left the prosecutor with the disagreeable task of executing the convicted felon himself,—both successful ways of discouraging litigation.

A good deal more modern than those barbarous practices, but still of a respectable antiquity, is the ducking-stool, resting on a transverse beam of the interior roofing. It is long since this engine for punishing scolds was used; not, perhaps, altogether by reason of gentler modern methods, nor that the feminine arts of scolding and nagging are decayed, but doubtless because the punishment was not effectual, and the last state of the nagged and henpecked, after the nagger and pecker had been ducked, was worse than the first. The old clumsy wooden crane at the angle of the town hall, still overlooking the river, was the place whence the scolding wives of Fordwich, first firmly bound, were slung in the chair, swung out over the stream, and ducked, deeply overhead. Raving with fear and shrieking with fury they were ducked again and again, while their good men, standing amid the delighted crowd, miserably anticipated a worse time than ever—and, by all accounts, generally got it.

STURRY.

Leaving Fordwich and returning to Sturry, the Canterbury road is regained. At its extremity, where one crosses the Stour, Sturry retrieves its reputation and exchanges its hard-featured street for a pretty riverside grouping, where the church, an ivy-covered ruined red-brick gateway of Sturry Court, and a plentiful background of trees make a gracious picture. It is the last picture of the kind on this route, for Canterbury is less than two miles ahead, entered past the barracks and by its least attractive streets.

CHAPTER XVII

THE ISLE OF SHEPPEY

Sheppey is an outlying district of the Ingoldsby Country, somewhat difficult of access. It is from Newington, a village on the Dover Road, some seven miles from Chatham and eighteen from Canterbury, that we will approach Sheppey, if cycling, for that affords a pleasant and interesting route. The ancient parish church of Newington lifts its grey battlemented tower away from the village prominently to one side of the old coach road, but it is surprisingly long before one reaches it, down the winding lane. Here it is abundantly evident, to right and left, that we are in the very heart of the famous fruit-growing district of Kent; for apple orchards, and more particularly cherry and pear orchards, abound, and where they cease the hop-gardens fill in the intervening space.

Coming sharply round to the church, incongruously neighboured by a modern and matter-of-fact postal letter-box, will be seen a great rough boulder-stone, planted between roadway and footpath—the "Devil's Stone" as it is known locally. A very large and prominent representation of a boot-sole is seen on it, and is the outward and visible sign of a hoary legend current at Newington ever since Newington church existed. It seems that the Devil objected to the church being built, but deferred action until the tower was completed, when, one night, he came along indignantly, and, placing his back against the tower and a foot against the stone, pushed—to no purpose, for the tower was not to be moved by his strongest efforts. The legend asks us to believe that the boot-print on the stone is a relic of this impotent Satanic spite; but it is in relief, instead of being sunk!—and surely the imprint, in any case, should have been that of a hoof. It is a very well-preserved and sharply-defined mark, and a suspicion that it is periodically renewed will not be denied.

THE DEVIL'S FOOTPRINT.

At any rate, it is an appropriate legend for the Ingoldsby Country. Had Barham only known of it, to what excellent use could he not have turned the tale!

Five miles of picturesquely winding sandy lanes lead in a gradual descent past Iwade, through orchards, and now and again across rough patches of open pasture, with two field-gates across the route, proclaiming that wayfarers here are few. At length a view of Sheppey opens out, across that arm of the sea known as the Swale, crossed by a combined railway and road bridge on the site of the old "King's Ferry." The railway is that branch of the Chatham and Dover running from Sittingbourne to Queenborough and Sheerness. Here then, paying the penny toll for self and cycle, one enters the island by road, at the only place where the channel is bridged. The four other places from which it is possible to enter are all ferries.

The railway to Sheerness has never opened up the island, and Sheppey, before the opening of the light railway that has recently been made to traverse its length, remained to Londoners an unknown land. It may be readily supposed that it will largely so remain, in spite of the facilities for travel that the new line provides, and notwithstanding the frantic efforts of the strenuous land companies, whose extravagant advertisements might lead the untravelled to suppose that here was the Garden of Eden, and that in purchasing building-sites in this remote corner of the kingdom speculators or prospective residents would be laying the foundations of rude health or comfortable fortunes. There are, it is true, few places so interesting as Sheppey, but why, apart from its history? Just because its scenery is so weird, its surroundings so outlandish. That scenery is of two sorts—the marshes that border the sea-channel of the

Swale, dividing it from the Kentish mainland; and the high ridge or backbone which runs in the direction of the island's greatest length, from Sheerness to Warden Point and Shellness. Trees are few, and grow only in the more sheltered parts, if it can truly be said that there is shelter at all on Sheppey, where the winds—particularly the east winds—blow great guns, and boom, howl, and shriek in successful competition with the cannon of the heavy defences at Sheerness, whose deep, hoarse voices are puny compared with those of the gales that blow on Sheppey. All these historic and physical peculiarities of this right little, tight little island are very well for the explorer, who goes forth to discover the unusual—and certainly finds it here—and who would be grievously disappointed at not finding it, but to live on Sheppey would be another matter. Those marshlands whose delicate tints and general air so appeal to the casual stranger in summer, that muddy sea which sullenly washes away the crumbling, slimy cliffs of dark clay along the coast-line from Sheerness to Warden, lose their interest in the long months of winter, become merely grim and dismal, and obsess the mind with doleful imaginings.

But these things have nothing to do with the literary pilgrim, who does not select the winter for his pilgrimage. He descends upon Sheppey in the summer, and here is the picture he sees, so soon as he has left the King's Ferry bridge behind. The road runs flatly and sandily ahead, in midst of a world of marshes, cloaked and successfully hidden for the most part by a luxuriant growth of grass. From a cloudless sky the song of the larks comes down in changeful trills, and if one dare gaze into the aching blue they can be seen, mounting higher and higher as though they sought to reach the sun itself. Everything else tells of noonday rest. The still heat that bathes the unduly energetic in undesirable perspiration sends one seeking for wayside shelter, but only on the distant hillside, where Minster crowns the ridge, do the trees begin, dotted singly, and looking in the distance like giant umbrellas. The myriad sheep of these flats have long since given up the quest for shade in this district where trees are only objects in the distance and hedgerows are unknown, and huddled together in an endeavour to find a cooling shade behind each other's backs. Even the lambs have ceased their clumsy gambols. The dykes stew in the sun, and a heat-haze makes distant objects in the landscape perform an optical St. Vitus's dance. Only the great brick-barges, beating up and down the creeks from Sittingbourne, go a slow and dignified pace, their rust-red sails, seen across country, looking as though they walked the fields. The colouring of this scene is in a beautiful harmony—the foreground grasses bleached to a more than straw-like pallor, toning off in the distance to a rich apricot yellow, meeting in one direction the irradiated pale blue sky, flecked with white clouds, and in another the green hillsides of

Minster. Over all is a sense of vastness, and the pilgrim throws out his arms and draws deep breaths in sympathy. Space, elbow-room, isolation, those are the dominant notes of Sheppey.

Queenborough, two miles off to the left from our entrance at King's Ferry, finds no mention in the *Ingoldsby Legends*, but now that we are here, a thorough exploration might as well be undertaken, and both it and Sheerness visited. Queenborough is a place with a past, and proclaims the fact in every nook and corner of its old streets, where the footfall of the stranger echoes loudly, and tufts of grass grow between the rough cobble-stones of the pavements. Queenborough owes its name to the chivalric courtesy of Edward III., who in 1366 changed it from Kingborough to its present title in honour of his Queen, Philippa. At that time it was an important point, and was fortified for the defence of the Medway by a castle designed by that master-architect and shrewd ecclesiastic, William of Wykeham. Archæologists tell how its ground-plan was in the shape of an heraldic rose, but nearly all traces of it are gone. Its history never included siege or stirring incident, and the buildings were ruinous even in the time of the Commonwealth, when they were sold and carted off in a commonplace and inglorious way. Now—the last note of humiliation—the railway station of Queenborough is built on the site.

The town dates the beginning of its decay from 1377, when Edward III. who had honoured it in the re-naming, eleven years before, ensured its ruin by removing the staple to Sandwich; but some life and enterprise would seem to have been left, even in the time of Queen Anne, for most of the houses in its one long street appear to have been built about the period of that deceased sovereign. Quaint red-brick houses they are, the brick seamed and pitted with age, the roofs high-pitched; the whole with that indefinite suggestion of a Dutch town which many of these old waterside ports possess, even though it be impossible to pick out one house and find anything particularly Dutch in its design.

It is not without a certain feeling of humiliation that one mentions anything Dutch along the Medway and in the neighbourhood of Sheerness, for Sheerness itself felt the brunt of the Dutch naval attack in June 1667, when seventy-two hostile ships reduced the little sandspit fort, landed a force, and occupied the town. Thence the Dutch Admiral at leisure proceeded up to Chatham, destroying the English ships and even working havoc in the Thames. Pepys at Gravesend remarked in his Diary, "We do plainly at this time hear the guns play,"—and in terror went off to Brampton, in Huntingdonshire, where he hid his wealth in an unlikely spot. It was not until the end of June that the fear of invasion was past, and no lapse of time has sufficed to wipe away the shame.

The dockyards and forts of Sheerness are to-day very efficient and formidable, but they do not succeed in rendering anything but an unfavourable opinion of the town, whose prevailing notes are meanness and squalor; few others than fishers or seafaring men of the Navy ever set foot here. It is the most considerable place on the island, and, the very Cinderella of dockyard towns, repels rather than invites the visitor.

Bluetown, an outlying residential part, overlooking the sea and possessed of a dwarf sea-wall and a parade of sorts, is better. Here the Government officials chiefly live, as it were, at the gates of the Unknown, for although there is nothing to hinder excursions into "the interior," few have ever been those to make the attempt. Looking at Sheppey with the eyes of Sheerness, one in fact regards that town largely in the light of a settlement on the coast of some impossible island in the most impossible of colonies. We shall, however, see that Sheppey contains more of interest in a day's tour than is readily to be found in the same time within the compass of the Home Counties.

For Sheppey—it is a redundancy to talk of the "Isle of Sheppey," the ancient Saxon "Sceapige," the "Isle of Sheep," including the designation of "island"—besides containing some of the most notable of Ingoldsby landmarks, has witnessed historic events. The outskirts of Sheerness are, of course, peculiarly soulless and abnormally gritty and dirty. If, however, the explorer perseveres until these are left behind, he will see in the distance, some two-and-a-half miles ahead, an isolated hill rising abruptly from the levels and surmounted by a Church. A nearer approach discovers a pretty countryside and the fact that an interesting village clings round the topmost slopes of the hill. This is the village of Minster-in-Sheppey, thus particularised in order to distinguish it from the better-known Minster-in-Thanet. The church was once a dependency of the abbey founded here by St. Saxburga, or Sexburga, in A.D. 675; the abbey spoken of in ancient documents as "Monasterium Scapeiæ," or "The Sheppey Monastery." It is this title that has given the village of Minster its name, as found in the changing forms of the word since the twelfth century, when it was "Moynstre." By degrees it became "Menstre," and thence assumed its present form. It is by no means proposed in these pages to follow the fortunes of Saxburga and her establishment of seventy-seven nuns, nor to tell the story of how the heathen Danes in after years desecrated the place. Sanctuaries existed in those times, it would seem (from the frequency and certainty of their being attacked) expressly for the purpose of being violated, and scarce a religious house, in the course of many centuries, escaped ruin at the hands of pagan piratical hordes, or of internal enemies who, although Christians, were hardly less savage. Even at a time so comparatively late as 1322, some tragical affair, whose details have never been disclosed, took place here, for at that time both the abbey and the church were said to have "suffered pollution from blood," and the Archbishop of Canterbury was entreated to send a faculty for holding a special service of reconciliation, to purge the place.

The abbey, of course, shared the common fate of such establishments, big and little, in the strenuous days of Henry VIII., and its buildings have been so diligently quarried for stone during more than three hundred years that nothing is left of them but the gatehouse, which neighbours the west end of the church. Even that has been ingeniously turned to account, and, with the great entrance archway bricked up, and modern sashed windows knocked into the walls, forms very comfortable quarters for the families of two farm-labourers.

But it is not to discuss abbesses, saintly or merely human, that we are here. Diligent readers of the *Ingoldsby Legends* will at once recognise Minster-in-Sheppey as the principal scene of one of the most interesting and humorous legends of the series, the prose story of "Grey Dolphin;" and not far distant is the site of Shurland Castle, where Sir Robert de Shurland, Lord of Shurland and Minster and Baron of Sheppey *in comitatu* Kent, dwelt, and, *teste* Tom Ingoldsby, "to the frame of a dwarf united the soul of a giant and the valour of a gamecock." There is, true enough, a great, clumsy altar-tomb in Minster church to the memory of that redoubtable Baron, who was a real person, and not one of Barham's "many inventions." And not only a real, but a very gallant and distinguished personage too, of whom it was perhaps rather too bad of Ingoldsby to draw so farcical a portrait. He took part in the Crusade of 1271, and was at a later period knighted by Prince Edward for gallantry at the siege of Caerlaverock. "If I were a young demoiselle," says an old romance, "I would give myself to that brave knight, Sir Robert de Shurland." Women ever loved brave men.

MINSTER-IN-SHEPPEY.

The effigy of the knight bespeaks a man rather tall and thin, than thick-set and of a dwarfish stature. The local tradition upon which Barham founded the

160

legend of "Grey Dolphin" is that the Lord of Shurland, happening to pass by the churchyard of Minster, found a fat friar in the act of refusing, unless he were paid for his services, to say the last rites of the Church over the body of a drowned sailor brought to this spot for burial. No one felt inclined to pay for the unfortunate mariner's passport to Heaven, and the friar was obdurate, refusing to accede to even the Baron's request. The Baron promptly slew the friar, and kicked his

body into the open grave, to bear the sailor company on his journey to Hades. Mother Church was not particularly fond of the greasy friars who at that time infested the country, but she could not brook so flagrant an insult; and accordingly, made matters extremely unpleasant for the Baron, who, learning that the King lay aboard ship two miles off the coast of Sheppey, swam there and back on his horse, Grey Dolphin, and obtained a pardon. But, on returning to the shore, an old woman prophesied that the horse which had now saved his life should some day cause his death. To render this, as he thought, impossible, the Baron killed his horse on the spot, and went off rejoicing. The next year, however, chancing to ride over the sands again, his horse stumbled over the skull of Grey Dolphin and threw the Baron fatally.

TOMB OF SIR ROBERT DE SHURLAND.

His tomb, rubbed down in a cleanly and housewifely manner quite destructive of any appearance of antiquity, is in the south aisle of Minster Abbey church —the effigy of a "recumbent warrior clad in the chain-mail of the thirteenth century. His hands are clasped in prayer; his legs, crossed in that position so prized by Templars in ancient and tailors in modern days, bespeak him a Soldier of the Faith in Palestine. Close behind his dexter calf lies sculptured in bold relief a horse's head." This is represented in the midst of some curious carving, perhaps intended for waves. At the feet of the mutilated effigy crouches a battered little figure of a page, misericorde in hand; while "Tickletoby," the Baron's sword, is represented in stone carving by his side, with a spear the length of his tomb. It was, as Tom Ingoldsby explains, "the fashion in feudal times to give names to swords: King Arthur's was christened Excalibur; the Baron called his Tickletoby, and whenever he took it in hand it was no joke." The legend of "Grey Dolphin" has been explained away by antiquaries, who say that the horse's head means only that Sir Robert de Shurland had obtained a grant of the "Wreck of the Sea" where his manors extended towards the shore, and was entitled to all wreckage, waifs and strays, flotsam and jetsam, which he could reach with the point of his lance when riding at ebb tide as far into the sea as possible.

The weather-vane on the tower, fashioned to represent a horse's head, alludes to this story, and gives the local name of the "Horse Church."

THE HORSE-VANE, MINSTER-IN-SHEPPEY.

The siege of Shurland Castle belongs more to fiction than to history, and it is only in Tom Ingoldsby's pages that you can read how Guy Pearson, one of the defenders, "had got a black eye from a brickbat." Most of the people—John de Northwode, William of Hever, and Roger of Leybourne—who led the assault are real persons, and, indeed, the brasses of Sir John de Northwode and his wife, Joan of Badlesmere, are there, in the church of Minster, to this day. Haines, the author of the first, and still the standard, work on *Monumental Brasses*, says the knight's effigy "has undergone a peculiar Procrustean process, several inches having been removed from the centre of the figure to make it equal in length to that of his wife. The legs have been restored and crossed at the ankles, an attitude apparently not contemplated by the original designer. From the style of engraving, these alterations seem to have been made at the close of the fifteenth century." Since Haines wrote, the brass of the knightly sheriff has been again restored, a piece of metal having been inserted, with the effect of lengthening the figure considerably. The effect of a modern slip of brass let into this fifteenth-century engraving is not a little incongruous.

The Baron who put John de Northwode and his *posse comitatus* to flight left a daughter, his sole heiress. If one could believe Ingoldsby (which one cannot do) it would be sufficient to read that "Margaret Shurland in due course became Margaret Ingoldsby; her portrait still hangs in the gallery at

163

Tappington. Her features are handsome but shrewish; but we never could learn that she actually kicked her husband." Diligent delving into old records proves, however, that Margaret Shurland married one William Cheyney; and the altar-tomb of their descendant, Sir Thomas Cheyney, Warden of the Cinque Ports in the time of good Queen Bess, stands in Minster church even now.

That noble monument details how important a personage he was. Knight of the Garter, Constable of Dover Castle, Treasurer of the Household to Henry VIII. and Edward VI., and Privy Councillor in the succeeding reigns of Mary and Elizabeth, he was obviously a man of affairs. Here the recumbent effigy of him lies, a surrounding galaxy of sixteen shields of arms setting forth the noble alliances of his house. He was a man of great wealth—probably he helped himself liberally out of the Treasury—and, razing Shurland Castle to the ground and leaving nothing to tell of the old stronghold, built in its stead the mansion now standing, but fallen from its old estate and become a farmhouse.

One marvels by what suavity of demeanour, what tact, double-dealing, and wholesale jettison of principles and personal convictions, political, social, and religious, this man of many dignities contrived to keep and augment his fortune and preserve his head upon his shoulders in the hurly-burly and general quick-change of those times in which he lived, when an incautious word meant Tower Hill and the executioner's axe, or, at the very least of it, the forfeiture of property. Surely he did not wear his heart upon his sleeve who moved thus freely in Courts, and who died, undisturbed and in the fulness of time, in his bed.

Minster church is rich in other monuments. Here in a recess of the wall can still be seen the mutilated alabaster effigy of a knight in armour, representing an unfortunate Spanish prisoner of rank captured by Drake off Calais harbour at the descent of the Armada in 1588. This poor Don Jeronimo Magno, of Salamanca, was given into the custody of Sir Edward Hoby, Constable of Queenborough and Commander at the Nore, who kept him for three years a prisoner aboard ship at that rough and boisterous anchorage. It is not surprising that the unhappy Jeronimo died at the end of that time—unless we like to be surprised that he stood it so long. He was buried here December 5th, 1591. The hooligan instincts of fanatical religious reformers, and still more those of the succeeding centuries of village goths and visitant 'Arrys, have bashed the nose of the effigy, shorn off at the elbow his once devoutly clasped arms, and scored him about with their quite uninteresting initials. Another such effigy, not so ill-treated, is that supposed to represent Jordanus de Scapeia, whose clasped hands still hold between their fingers a mystic oval sculptured with a little effigy thought to symbolise the soul. This monument was found buried in the churchyard, in 1833, five feet deep.

THE SOUL, FROM A MONUMENT IN MINSTER-IN-SHEPPEY CHURCH.

From this hilltop churchyard one may glimpse a view whose like is not often seen. Sheerness to one side, the narrow ribbon of the Swale, the broad channels of the Medway and the Thames, and the great expanse of slimy marshes, gleam under the summer sun like burnished steel. When evening comes and the sunbeams slant downwards from dun-coloured clouds, the scene is one to make an artist despair of ever adequately rendering the beauty of it.

The dust of countless generations lies mingled here, in this swelling God's Acre, raised so high above the road. Abbesses and nuns and the good folks of Minster for many hundreds of years have all found rest at last, and most of their names are forgotten, save by the casual antiquary who turns over the yellow pages of the parish registers. Most of the gravestones date from periods ranging from a hundred to sixty years ago, and their inscriptions tell eloquently of a seafaring population near at hand—at Sheerness, of course; for the ship's carpenters, rope-makers, boatswains, master-mariners, and the many others of the seafaring profession generally have their occupation duly set forth on their memorials. The rope-maker's is embellished with ropes, curiously carved and fashioned, representing knots whose name sailormen alone may know. Others bear terrific attempts at picturing the Judgment Day, intended to make the casual sinner quail. Unfortunately, the puffy, overfed angels blowing the Last Trump on trumpets many sizes too large for them make the sinful smile, and they go away quite undisturbed in their old iniquitous ways.

So greatly has the soil of the churchyard been raised by the countless years of interments, that the church itself lies, as it were, in a little hollow, and the entrances to it by the south door, and from the western portal in the tower, are flanked by walls of grassy earth, the whole immediately overlooking and abutting upon the houses of the homely village.

THE ESTUARY OF THE MEDWAY, FROM THE ROAD NEAR MINSTER-IN-SHEPPEY.

There are exquisitely beautiful glimpses on the road from Minster to Warden, beginning immediately on leaving the place. To the left, a lovely valley that in Devonshire would be called a "coombe," and in the Isle of Wight a "chine," shelves down to the sea at the farm of Scrapsgate. There from the road you see the valley, notched out like a **V**, with myriads of wild-flowers, and in the distance on the right hand the farm-buildings, nestling among orchards and a dense clump of trees, and in that wedge of the **V** the sparkling waters of a sea that is always alive and companionable with the great steamers coming in or out of the mouth of

the Thames, with the brick-lighters and sailing-barges creeping round the island, or with the swallow-like flight of the graceful yachts of the Royal Thames Yacht Squadron. Turning in the other direction, the mazy creeks and many islands and saltings of the Medway are stretched out, silver-grey and opalescent, over beyond the shoulder of the hill—mystic, wonderful, sanctified by distance to the likeness of a Promised Land.

In two miles from Minster we come to Eastchurch, a populous and pretty village whose beautiful church warms the enthusiasm of the pilgrim. Across the meadows rises the imposing frontage of Shurland House, now, as we have said, a farmhouse, but a Gothic battlemented structure built by Sir Thomas Cheyney, when Warden of the Cinque Ports, about 1550, and the not undignified successor of the Shurland Castle inhabited by that Sir Robert who was the hero of the legend of "Grey Dolphin."

Sir Thomas, the builder of this great place, was succeeded by his son, "the extravagant Lord Cheyney" of Toddington, Bedfordshire, after whose fall Shurland House reverted to the Crown. James I. granted it to Philip Herbert, a son of the Earl of Pembroke, and now, after many vicissitudes, it belongs to the Holfords.

SHURLAND CASTLE.

By turning to the left in the village street of Eastchurch, and bearing to the right at the next turning, all that is left of Warden is reached in two miles. The little that remains of the village is known by the inelegant name of "Mud Row," whose few decrepit houses lead direct to what would be destruction for the speedy cyclist, were it not for the rough bar thrown across the rutty lane.

Dismounting here, the astonished stranger finds that the road ends suddenly and without warning, and with it the island as well. It is just a little nerve-shaking. Here one looks down upon a scene of wildest desolation, upon the sea, a hundred feet below, at the bottom of a dark mass of clayey cliffs, slipping and sliding into the water, and torn by repeated landslips into yawning fissures and fantastic pinnacles. The sullen sea is discoloured as far as eye can reach with the dissolving clay, and, horrible to tell, out of many fissures grin bleached skulls, while strewn here and there are human bones. It is a Golgotha. Here stood the church and churchyard of Warden until 1877, and this tumbled landslip is all that remains of them.

For many years this encroachment of the sea at Warden has been in progress, until, up to now, over eighty acres have been washed away. The vanished church has a curious history, having been rebuilt in 1836 with the stones from old London Bridge, demolished four years earlier for the building of the present structure. It was Delamark Banks, son of Sir Edward Banks, the contractor for the bridge, who gave the stones and rebuilt the church of Warden, as duly set forth on a sculptured stone tablet now forming part of a garden wall at Mud Row.

By 1870 the sea had crept up to the church, and it was closed, to be pulled down in 1877, when the bodies of those who had been buried in the churchyard during the previous thirty years were disinterred and removed to Minster. They are the more ancient dead whose poor remains are exposed with every fall of earth, to bleach in the sun.

From the desolation of Warden it is four miles to that hooked spit of shells and sand, Shellness, the farthest extremity of the island. By tracks which might, with every excuse, be described as hazardous, the route begins, but soon descends to the low sea-shore and the flat marshes—the shore carefully protected by a long series of dwarf timber groynes and a curved "apron" of concrete, the marshes defended by massive earthen dykes, continued along the circuitous shore all the way round to King's Ferry.

Shellness is well named, for it is a vast expanse of small marine shells, mostly in a perfect condition. Such a beach would be the paradise of holiday children at a seaside resort, but here, at the edge of an obscure island, where there is no life but that of a coastguard station and the nearest village is almost three miles away, it is clearly wasted. Among this wilderness of shells grows the beautiful yellow sea-poppy, finding its nutriment in some mysterious manner where no soil can be seen.

Three miles across the sea-channel of the Swale lies Whitstable, plain to see, and in the Swale rides the oyster fleet of that celebrated fishery.

This channel of the Swale was the point of departure selected by James II. when flying, terror-stricken, before the Protestant deliverance of the nation by William of Orange. It was in December 1688 that a hoy was chartered and the fugitive King landed at Elmley, higher up the channel, intending to put off from this point or hook of Shellness; but the unwonted spectacle of a humble boat containing persons in the garb of great gentlemen landing in that obscure place in those troubled times created a sensation among the fishermen, who took them for Jesuits, and, hating Popery and eager for plunder, mobbed them. They thought the King was that notorious Jesuit, Father Petre. "I know him by his lean jaws," said one. "Search the hatchet-faced old Jesuit!" exclaimed another. They snatched his money and watch; his coronation ring and valuable trinkets—even the diamond buckles of his shoes—they took for glass and did not touch.

Then—tremendous discovery!—someone recognised him as the King. A momentary awe seized them, but they quickly recovered, and this poor trembling James they took, incoherently protesting, in custody across the Swale and into Faversham, there to be placed under surveillance.

This is why this corner of Sheppey is interesting. It witnessed one of the final scenes in the tragedy of the Stuarts.

CHAPTER XVIII

SOME OUTLYING INGOLDSBY LANDMARKS

NETLEY ABBEY

Three miles from Southampton, in the county of Hampshire—or, as official documents still have it, the county of Southampton—is Netley Abbey, one of the scattered Ingoldsby landmarks outside Kent. It is not evident from the context in the Legends when or on what occasion the author visited Netley, nor does it appear to be explained in the "Life" by his son. The ruined abbey stands almost on the shores of Southampton Water, divided from that beautiful land and seascape only by a road and the gardens of a narrow fringe of villas. The site is naturally lovely, but has been spoiled and vulgarised by the neighbourhood of the great military hospital and the draggle-tailed, unkempt, and sordid line of mean shops and public-houses which that institution has conjured up. So surely as Government buildings—be they hospitals, offices, barracks, or prisons—are erected on any spot, that spot is certain to be spoiled, and this is assuredly no exception. Stucco-fronted public-houses of the "Prince Albert" and "Hero of the Alma" type and period jostle the struggling, compendious greengrocer's shop that deals at one and the same time in greengrocery, half a hundred weight of coals, firewood, and linen drapery, and the picnicker comes in crowds to the spot on Southampton's early-closing days.

How different this from Horace Walpole's description of the place in 1755: "How shall I describe Netley to you? I can only by telling you it is the spot in the world which I and Mr. Chute wish. The ruins are vast, and retain fragments of beautiful fretted roof pendent in the air, with all variety of Gothic patterns of windows wrapped round and round with ivy. Many trees are sprouted up among the walls, and only want to be increased with cypresses. A hill rises above the abbey, encircled with wood. The fort, in which we would build a tower for habitation, remains, with two small platforms. This little castle is buried from the abbey in a wood, in the very centre, on the edge of the hill. On each side breaks in the view of the Southampton sea, deep blue, glistening with silver and vessels; on one side terminated by Southampton, on the other by Calshot Castle, and the Isle of Wight rising above the opposite hills. In short, they are not the ruins of Netley, but of Paradise. Oh! the purple abbots! what a spot had they chosen to slumber in! The scene is so beautifully tranquil, yet so lively, that they seem only to have retired *into* the world."

There are various derivations of the name of Netley, but the true one is doubtless from the Anglo-Saxon "Natanleage," a wooded district. Other "Netleys" occur in the New Forest, and the name compares curiously with that of the little hamlet of "Nately Scures," near Basingstoke, where the suffix derives from the Anglo-Saxon "scora," a shaw or coppice. The abbey was a Cistercian house founded in the reign of, and perhaps by, Henry III., who dedicated it not only to the Virgin Mary, to whom Cistercian houses were always inscribed, but also to his patron saint, Edward the Confessor. The beautiful abbey church escaped the usual fate which befell religious houses at the Dissolution, and remained practically uninjured until so late as the year 1700. Up to that period it had passed through several hands, and although converted into a private residence, with the nave as a kitchen and the other hitherto sacred precincts turned into account for more or less domestic use, the successive owners had allowed no spoliation of its architectural features. But when in 1700 it became the property of Sir Berkeley Lucy, its doom was sealed. He sold the materials of the church to a certain Taylor, a Southampton builder, and Taylor made arrangements to pull the great building down. But Taylor, like Joseph, had a dream. He dreamt that, while engaged in taking down the church roof, the keystone of the vaulting near the great east window fell from its place and killed him. The dream probably had its origin in the warnings that had been given him by superstitious friends some days before, not to touch the abbey with the hands of a spoiler. They would not, they said, for riches untold "be concerned in the demolition of holy and consecrated places." Taylor was equally superstitious and the warning preyed upon his mind, and the dream was the result. The next day he hurried off to another friend, a Mr. Watts, schoolmaster in Southampton and the father of that celebrated divine Dr. Isaac Watts, author of "How doth the little busy bee" and other improving verse. Mr. Watts, schoolmaster, seems to have been an unworthy progenitor of that highly moral cleric, and gave the troubled Taylor the cynical advice "to have no personal concern in pulling down the building." This admirable, if somewhat forbiddingly rationalistic, counsel was, however, disregarded by the unhappy contractor, who, when actively engaged among his workmen was felled to the ground exactly in the manner he had dreamt. The falling keystone crushed his skull in, and the genius of the place was thus avenged. The workmen, who had heard the story of the dream and had laughed at it, then left off work in terror, and no one else was found bold enough to proceed with it. To this we owe the fact that the ruins are still in existence, but it seems a pity that the vengeful spirit could have found no method of getting his blow in before the abbey was almost wholly unroofed. Had Taylor been slain by the first stone wrenched from the groining the swiftness of the retribution would have rendered it even more dramatic, and would have resulted in the beautiful building being roofed to this day.

NETLEY ABBEY.

As it is, the ruins are now open to the sky, and time and the seasons have wrought more havoc in the two centuries that have passed than was inflicted by Taylor or his men. Time, weather, and vandal visitors, that is to say—these last we must by no means forget. Not that they are likely to be forgotten by the pilgrim to this shrine, for the walls are hacked and inscribed with the pocket-knives and pencils of two centuries of holiday-makers, pricked

on to it by a noble rage for immortality manifesting itself in this ignoble way. The earlier scrawls of John Jones or William Robinson have themselves, almost by lapse of time, come within the range of archæology. From 1700 to about 1860 these, almost as destructive as the tooth of time, had their wicked will of the place, and it was under such circumstances and the added desecrations of bottled beer, drunken fiddling, and rowdy picnicking, that Barham saw it:

> In a rush-bottom'd chair
> A hag surrounded by crockery-ware,
> Vending in cups to the credulous throng,
> A nasty decoction miscall'd Souchong,—
> And a squeaking fiddle and wry-neck'd fife
> Are screeching away, for the life!—for the life!
> Danced to by "All the World and his Wife."
> Tag, Rag, and Bobtail are capering there,
> Worse scene, I ween, than Bartlemy Fair!—
> Two or three Chimney-sweeps, two or three Clowns,
> Playing at "pitch and toss," sport their "Browns";
> Two or three damsels, frank and free,
> Are ogling and smiling, and sipping Bohea.

Parties below, and parties above,
Some making tea, and some making love.
    Then the "toot-toot-toot"
    Of that vile demi-flute,—
    The detestable din Of that crack'd violin,
And the odours of "Stout," and tobacco, and gin.
"Dear me!" I exclaimed, "what a place to be in!"

Since the dawning of the 'sixties, a better taste has prevailed, and
promiscuous jollification has been checked alike by the levying of an entrance
fee and by an improvement in manners; but the providing of teas within the
ruins is objectionable, and the *quality* of the "Souchong" and its
accompanying sawdusty cake might easily be better—it could not possibly be
worse.

It is best to visit Netley when the crowd may reasonably be expected to have
left. At such a time, shortly before sunset, the spot is most impressive. The
jackdaws, who seem to have the right of domicile in all ruinated buildings,
have gone, clamorous, to bed in the chinks of wall and airy gable, and one
shares the smooth lawns only with the robins, whose pretty confidence in the
harmlessness of human beings is the most touching thing in so-called "wild"
nature. The first stanza of Barham's poem is excellently descriptive of the
time and place, save that "roofless tower" is a poetic figure unwarranted by
facts—Netley Abbey has no towers:

    I saw thee, Netley, as the sun
        Across the western wave
    Was sinking slow, And a golden glow
        To thy roofless tower he gave;
    And the ivy sheen, With its mantle of green
        That wrapt thy walls around,
    Shone lovelily bright, In that glorious light,
        And I felt 'twas holy ground.

He then goes on to enlarge upon the legend of a refractory nun having been
walled up alive in the abbey, and to meditate upon the justice of Heaven fallen
upon Netley in the time of Henry VIII.:

    Ruthless Tudor's bloated form
    Rides on the blast and guides the storm.[A]

The context gives the date of the ruin of the fabric as at that period; but we
have already seen that this took place quite a hundred and sixty years later.
The curious, too, might ask what the nun was doing in a Cistercian monastery.
It is not a little singular to note that Barham has made no use, and indeed no

mention, of the picturesque legend of Taylor's death.

[A] *cf.* "Rides on the whirlwind and directs the storm."

THE DEAD DRUMMER

A LEGEND OF SALISBURY PLAIN

Oh, Salisbury Plain is bleak and bare,—
At least so I've heard many people declare,
For I fairly confess I never was there:—
Not a shrub, nor a tree, Nor a bush can you see,
No hedges, no ditches, no gates, no stiles,
Much less a house or a cottage for miles;
—It's a very sad thing to be caught in the rain
When night's coming on upon Salisbury Plain.

Salisbury Plain is, as Ingoldsby rightly assures us, bleak and barren. It is remarkable to note that, although as he truly says in the legend itself he was never there, he catches exactly the spirit of that dreary Wiltshire table-land, and describes it with such insight, picturesqueness, and economy of words and space as never at any other time have been used to give a proper mental picture of that vast solitude. It is far removed from the Ingoldsby Country proper, and might easily have been more loosely described in those opening lines; but they are perfect, alike topographically and for the production of that mental picture required to start the tale of horror.

The exact spot on the plain described in the legend where the two sailors, overtaken by the storm, vainly seek shelter, and where the vision of the dead drummer appears, can, thanks to the precision of the verse, be readily found. It is in the central and wildest spot of the wilderness, two miles almost due east of the small village of Tilshead. Let us here refer to the legend:

But the deuce of a screen, Could be anywhere seen
Or an object except that, on one of the rises,
An old way-post show'd Where the Lavington road
Branch'd off to the left from the one to Devizes.

Black Down the surrounding expanse is named. Bare and bleak, the close grass a wan sage-green, the white road divides across the treeless undulations, with a signpost directing right and left to Devizes and Lavington, exactly as described. But alterations are now in the making, and when completed will thoroughly alter and abolish the solitude of the place. "They have spoiled my battlefield," exclaimed the Duke of Wellington when he revisited Waterloo and found it stuck full of monuments; and the "East Camp" on the right of this spot, and the "West Camp" on the left, with all the permanent buildings and the great masses of troops now established on the plain, are changing it

173

beyond recognition. Where the bustard lingered longest and the infrequent traveller came timorously, the bugles blow and crowded battalions manœuvre every day.

But the true story of the dead drummer is very different from Ingoldsby's version. He has taken many liberties, both as regards scene and names, with the real facts of a remarkable case—for the legend is founded upon facts.

SALISBURY PLAIN: WHERE THE LAVINGTON ROAD BRANCHES OFF TO THE LEFT FROM THE ONE TO DEVIZES.

It seems that on Thursday, June 15th, 1786, two sailors paid off from H.M.S. *Sampson* at Plymouth came tramping up to London along the old Exeter Road. Their names were Gervase (or Jarvis) Matcham and John Shepherd. They came nowhere near Salisbury Plain, but pursued their course direct along the old coach road from Blandford towards Salisbury. Near the "Woodyates Inn" they were overtaken by a thunderstorm, when Matcham startled his messmate by showing extraordinary signs of horror and distracted faculties, running to and fro, falling on his knees, and imploring mercy of some invisible enemy. To his companion's questions he answered that he saw several strange and dismal spectres, particularly one in the shape of a woman, towards which he advanced, when it instantly sank into the earth and a large stone rose up in its place. Other large stones also rolled upon the ground before him, and came dashing against his feet. There can be no doubt that both Matcham and Shepherd were unnerved by the violence of the thunder and lightning, and that the terror of Matcham, who had very special reasons for fright, communicated itself to his friend to such a degree that when Matcham's diseased imagination saw moving shapes which had no existence, Shepherd readily saw them also. Thus, when the terrified Matcham fancied he

174

saw numbers of stones with glaring eyes turn over and keep pace with them along the road, Shepherd very soon became afflicted with what specialists in mental phenomena term "collective hallucination."

They then agreed to walk on either side of the road, and so perceive, by the behaviour of the stones, which of them it was who had so affronted God. The stones then exclusively accompanied Matcham all the way to the inn, where he beheld the Saviour and the drummer-boy, very terrible and accusing. To the roll of a drum, and in a terrific flash of lightning, they dissolved into dust.

Thereupon, overcome by these terrors, Matcham made confession there and then to Shepherd of a murder he had committed six years earlier, on the Great North Road, and begged his companion to hand him over to the nearest magistrate, in order that the avenging spectres and justice might be satisfied. He was accordingly committed at Salisbury pending inquiries as to the truth of his confession.

Those inquiries disclosed a remarkable story. Matcham, it appeared, was the son of a farmer of Frodingham, Yorkshire. When in his twelfth year he had run away from home and became a jockey. In the course of this employment he was despatched to Russia, in charge of some horses sent by the Duke of Northumberland to the Empress, and, returning to London well supplied with money, dissipated it all in evil courses. He then shipped as a sailor on board the *Medway* man-o'-war, but after a short experience of fighting managed to desert. He had no sooner landed in England after this escapade than he was seized by one of the pressgangs then scouring the seaports, and shipped aboard the *Ariadne*. Succeeding, when off Yarmouth, in an attempt to escape, he enlisted in the 13th Regiment of Foot, but, deserting again near Chatham, set out to tramp home, through London, to Yorkshire, passing Huntingdon on the way. The 49th Regiment was then recruiting in that district, and this extraordinary Matcham promptly enlisted in it.

Shortly after having joined, he was sent on the morning of August 19th, 1780, from Huntingdon to Diddington, five miles distant, to draw some subsistence-money, between six and seven pounds, from a Major Reynolds. With him went a drummer-boy, Benjamin Jones, aged about sixteen, son of the recruiting sergeant. Having drawn the money, they returned along the high-road. Instead of turning off to Huntingdon, Matcham induced the boy to go on with him in the direction of Alconbury, and picking a quarrel with him because he refused to stop and drink at a wayside public-house, knocked him down at a lonely spot still known as "Matcham's Bridge" and cut his throat there. He then made off with the money to London, leaving the body by the roadside. Shipping again in the Navy, he saw six years of hard fighting under Rodney and Hood, being finally paid off, as at first described.

In the contemporary account of this remarkable affair, taken down from Matcham's own statements by the chaplain of the gaol at Huntingdon, whither he was conveyed for trial from Salisbury, he stated that he was drunk at the time when the crime was committed, and did it, being suddenly instigated by the Devil, without any premeditated design. Further, that he had never afterwards had a single day's peace of mind. He was duly found guilty, and executed on August 2nd, 1786, his body being afterwards gibbeted on Alconbury Hill.

Lightning Source UK Ltd.
Milton Keynes UK
UKHW041043100820
367987UK00004B/957